The Robot's Revenge

Suddenly Frank and Joe heard a strange combination of clicking and pounding. Something was crashing down the aisle toward them.

Joe's breath stopped when he saw a huge brown dog leaping toward his friend Phil. The mutt growled ferociously as it flew through the air.

"Hit the ground!" Joe cried, shoving Phil in the back. When the huge dog saw its target go down, it flailed its legs and landed heavily on the table. Foam dripped from its muzzle as it snarled, looking for new prey.

"Nice little puppy dog," Joe murmured, trying to soothe the beast.

Frank glanced at Joe. Both of them knew the only way out was past the table, past the dog. "There's nowhere to go!" Frank yelled.

The dog sank down into an attack position. It was poised to spring—straight for Joe's throat!

The Hardy Boys
Mystery Stories

Available from MINSTREL Books

123

The
HARDY
BOYS®

THE ROBOT'S
REVENGE

FRANKLIN W. DIXON

A
MINSTREL®
BOOK

PUBLISHED BY POCKET BOOKS

New York   London   Toronto   Sydney   Tokyo   Singapore

A MINSTREL PAPERBACK *ORIGINAL*

A Minstrel Book published by
POCKET BOOKS, a division of Simon & Schuster Inc.
1230 Avenue of the Americas, New York, NY 10020

Copyright © 1993 by Simon & Schuster Inc.
Front cover illustration by Daniel Horne

Produced by Mega-Books of New York, Inc.

ISBN: 0-671-79313-6

First Minstrel Books printing December 1993

10 9 8 7 6 5 4 3 2

THE HARDY BOYS MYSTERY STORIES is a trademark
of Simon & Schuster Inc.

THE HARDY BOYS, A MINSTREL BOOK, and colophon
are registered trademarks of Simon & Schuster Inc.

Printed in the U.S.A.

Contents

THE ROBOT'S
REVENGE

1 Dog Days

"Where's his head?" Joe Hardy asked frantically. He glanced at his watch, then dropped to his knees and hastily searched under the table.

"We'll find it," Frank said from the corner of the exhibition booth. Joe's brother, Frank, and their friend Phil Cohen were crouched on the floor, furiously grabbing pieces from a pile of odd-shaped fiberglass and metal.

Putting a neon green torque wrench down on the hardwood floor, Frank looked over his shoulder at Joe and tried to stay calm. Even so, beads of sweat began to form along Frank's hairline.

Joe scowled. He felt frustrated, hungry, and tired. Everything had gone wrong for the trio on their trip from Bayport, including the terrible weather that made their plane land in Chicago several hours late. They had to race to set up before the hall closed for the night.

"Well, it's your invention, not mine," Joe said, running grimy fingers through his blond hair. "Don't you know where you put the head?" Getting no answer from his brother, Joe grumbled and sank down onto his and Frank's army surplus duffel bag.

Immediately Joe leapt up as if he'd been stung. "Hey!" he yelled. He turned around and knelt down by the duffel.

Frank and Phil turned in surprise to see the seventeen-year-old rummaging through the bag. As he threw a Knicks sweatshirt out onto the gym floor with his right hand, he reached into the duffel with his left and yanked out a metallic object shaped like a bicycle helmet.

"Roger's head!" Joe exclaimed. Smiling triumphantly, he held it up for his friends to see. Roger the Lobber's eyes stared at the guys silently.

"Oh . . . yes . . . right . . ." Phil murmured. He pushed his brown hair out of his eyes.

Both Hardys looked at their friend. Phil was an electronics whiz and had helped them with many of their technical problems during investigations. Frank and Joe had followed their father's footsteps in fighting crime. Years ago Fenton Hardy had retired from the New York City police force to become a private investigator. His sons had learned the business by working with their father and had solved many cases on their own, too, all over the world. Phil was always eager to help the Hardys on a case, but at the moment he felt a little sheepish.

"Guys, I'm sorry," Phil said. "I stuck Roger's head in your duffel before we left Bayport. After all those last-minute adjustments, we were in such a hurry to catch the plane that I didn't have time to fit it in the carrying case."

Joe studied Phil. "You knew where the head was the whole time? And you just *forgot*? Maybe you're the one who's lost his head."

"Lighten up, Joe," Frank said.

Phil shrugged and handed Frank the aluminum arm from the black carrying case. The case, which was covered with decals and bumper stickers, was one of the neatest things about the robot. It was carefully constructed from an old steamer trunk so that all thirty-eight parts of Roger the Lobber fit in perfectly. The case had wheels so the robot traveled easily. The robot could be taken apart or whipped together in under ten minutes. Together, Frank and Phil attached the arm to Roger's trunk.

A few minutes later, Joe's blue eyes were calmer. "Hey, here are the wheels," he said, digging under the pile of tools. Frank connected both of the foot-long tracks of bright purple rubber in-line skate wheels to an axle underneath Roger's body.

"Ready to try out our little buddy?" Frank

3

asked as he hooked the last wire up on the circuit board. He gave Roger a friendly pat, then tossed Phil the remote control and a specially treated orange tennis ball.

Phil threw the ball into the corner of their booth. Then he punched a button marked Fetch on the controller.

Roger started buzzing. Its head spun in a circle, stopping when its "mouth"—the blinking red remote in its head—picked up the sensor on the ball. The robot rolled over to the corner and sucked up the ball with the adapted vacuum cleaner hose at the end of its arm.

"Okay, Roger, show us the rest," Phil commanded, moving a lever on the controller.

The robot turned to Phil and spit the ball out of a compartment in the upper part of its bottom section. Joe reached over and intercepted the ball before it got to Phil.

"Tennis ace Joe Hardy nabs the volley with some awesome net play!" Joe exclaimed. The younger Hardy placed the ball on the table and started out into the aisle. "Roger the Lobber is ready for the competition—as long as it isn't coming from me. Let's check the rest of the competition."

Frank glanced at his watch. "Not bad! Thirteen minutes before closing." He looked at Joe, who was leaning against the booth divider tapping his fingers. "We can't look at the other stuff until we check in at the TIC booth."

4

The initials stood for Teen Inventors' Club. Frank pulled out the floor plan of the competitors' booths, which were set up in the gymnasium of Cahill College, in Chicago. There were almost a hundred student inventors in ten side aisles. A wide center aisle connected the two doors at either end of the gym. "Check-in desk is at the front," Frank noted.

Joe shrugged. "Fine, so let's go check in," he said with an edge to his voice.

Frank looked sideways at him. "Why are you so keyed up?" he asked.

Joe flushed, then grinned weakly. "I guess I'm jealous. I wish I had gone in on the Roger the Lobber project with you and Phil. This inventors' convention is totally cool."

"And you thought we were a couple of nerds," Frank said, lightly punching his brother in the arm. "Just think. We nerds have the opportunity to win a college scholarship, get our inventions produced and sold by well-known companies, and work for these companies as interns."

"No need to rub it—" Joe began.

Phil interrupted, "Yeah, well, we nerds aren't going to get to compete at all if we don't get over to the registration booth."

The three guys filed out of their booth, the last one in that aisle, and headed for the registration booth. Joe left his friends there and wandered off to look around.

Frank and Phil registered quickly, then went

after Joe. When they caught up with him, he was examining an automatic glass sorter for recycling.

"Check this out!" he exclaimed when Frank and Phil walked up. "The glass goes down this conveyor belt and through a light beam. The darker the glass is, the less light passes through. The machine tells what color the glass is by sensing how much light goes through. Then the conveyor belt just drops the bottle into the proper container. It's great."

Frank laughed. "We'll make a nerd out of you yet, bro. Hey! We've got time to look around now. The hall isn't closing for another hour. The weather's so crummy that a lot of the inventors, not to mention some of the judges, have been delayed."

"They're going to let people check in and set up tonight and again tomorrow morning, right up until the expo starts," Phil added.

"Huh. I guess that explains why there aren't that many people here," Joe said, looking around the quiet gymnasium. "Come on, let's see some more stuff."

In the next aisle, the Hardys examined a surfboard that folded up to the size of a briefcase and a backpack that converted into a sleeping bag. Phil wandered off down one of the other aisles.

As the brothers came to the center aisle, Frank pointed out a booth with a sleek black computer set up on a stand. "That booth belongs to one of the sponsoring corporations, Sobba. Phil says

6

they're the top computer company in Europe. They've got this new voice-sensitive computer—I bet that's a demo model."

Joe whistled. "Now, this we have to see."

Joe peered over his brother's shoulder as Frank started talking to the computer. After a little experimenting, Frank looked up. "No keyboard, no mouse, no anything. This thing is incredible!" he said. "I'd love to have one."

After almost an hour of looking, Phil had just come back. "Dream on," he said, chuckling. "They cost more than any of us can afford." He stuffed half a candy bar into his mouth, crunched, then swallowed it in a froglike gulp. "Let's go grab our bags. The place is going to close in a few minutes."

"And I'm starved," Joe chimed in. He gazed longingly at the other half of Phil's candy bar. "Where'd you get that?"

"There are machines back that way," Phil said, waving his hand vaguely. As they walked back to their booth, he went on, "I just saw a really cool invention. This guy, I think his name is Byron, made a stationery maker. Not just plain paper, but the pretty kind that has a texture. The great thing, though, is that Byron uses old newspapers as the raw material for the stationery."

"So it recycles newspapers into something you can actually use. Good idea. Our old papers are always piling up," Frank commented.

"Hey, look, our neighbor across the aisle has

7

arrived," Joe said. "There's a pile of stuff in the back of the booth."

Frank read the sign dangling from her booth divider. "Megan Sweetwater. Hobbs, New Mexico. We'll have to wait until tomorrow to find out what she's got. We need to pick up and get out of here if we want to shower before the welcome cruise."

Phil looked around the booth. "Wait, do either of you see Roger's ball? I thought it was on the table before."

Frank and Joe both shook their heads as they scanned the nearby area.

"Let Roger get it," Joe suggested. He picked up the remote control and touched the Fetch button. Frank got ready to grab the robot in case it rolled into something. The one thing he and Phil hadn't been able to figure out was how to make the robot avoid things in its path. But on a tennis court they wouldn't have that problem.

The robot whirled its head a couple times, hummed a little, and rolled straight across the aisle, through Megan Sweetwater's booth entrance and into the pile of stuff at the back.

"I don't see the ball. It looks like Roger's having trouble," Frank said as he watched the robot get tangled in the pile of clothing. "I bet the ball's under those sweats."

He walked toward the pile, stooped, and pulled the ball from under the clothes. "Yup, it's under this sweatshirt. Figures. There's no other way we all could miss a bright orange ball," he said, standing up again.

"Hey, what's this?" Joe crossed over and pulled something out from behind a small suitcase. It was a wide, woven nylon belt with several buttons and dials surrounding the buckle.

"Looks like a weight lifter's back support belt. I wonder what all the controls do?" Frank bounced the tennis ball as he spoke.

Phil laughed from the booth entrance. "Maybe this person has invented a new way to lose weight. You put it on, and it squeezes the fat off—kind of an electronic girdle." Joe and Frank joined their friend's laughter.

At that moment the boys heard a strange combination of clicking and pounding on the hardwood floor. Something was crashing down the aisle toward the end booths.

"What the—?" Phil muttered, as he leaned out into the aisle. Joe stepped up behind him.

His breath stopped when he saw the huge brown dog leaping toward Phil. The mutt growled ferociously as it flew through the air.

"Hit the ground!" Joe yelled, shoving Phil in the back. Phil dropped onto the floor on his stomach. Joe threw himself backward into the corner as Frank dived into the pile of clothing at the back of the booth.

When the huge dog saw its target go down, it flailed its legs and landed heavily on the booth table. Foam dripped from its muzzle as it snarled, looking for new prey. Regaining its balance, it stood on the edge of the table, eyeing the Hardys.

"Nice little puppy dog," Joe said, trying to soothe the beast.

Frank risked a glance at Joe. Both of them knew the only way out of the booth was past the table and the dog. "There's nowhere to go!" Frank cried.

The dog backed up the six inches to the far edge of the table. It sank down into an attack position. It was poised to spring—straight for Joe's throat.

2 Accusations Fly

"Good dog. Sit," Frank murmured, trying to buy time. "That's a good puppy." The mutt turned its head slightly and growled at Frank. The hair on the back of its neck rose even higher.

"Joe," Phil whispered. Joe was crawling to a squatting position in the aisle, trying to slowly inch his way away from the dog.

"The remote! Use the remote!" Phil hissed.

Frank immediately understood what Phil meant. Still murmuring to the dog, Frank reached over himself to the robot and slowly unwrapped Roger's wheels, which were tangled in the sweatshirt.

Meanwhile, Joe worked Roger's remote out of his jeans pocket. Out of the corner of his eyes, Joe saw that Roger was free to move.

"Now, Joe!" Phil cried. At the same time, Frank tossed the tennis ball toward their own booth.

Joe hit the Fetch button on the control panel. When the robot's head started to spin and blink, a long growl came out of the dog. The huge animal jumped up to a sitting position, cocked its head at the robot, and stared suspiciously.

When Roger began to roll toward the table, the dog dropped its tail between its legs and started backing up. As the robot got closer, the whimpering beast moved back faster.

The robot plowed into the table. The dog scooted backward. Both it and the table crashed to the floor. Yelping, the dog turned to run.

Suddenly a girl's voice yelled, "What are you doing to my dog?"

Joe spun around. A dark-haired girl was sprinting toward the booth. When the dog heard her, it ran over to her side, wagging its tail.

"Bunny, are you all right?" she said softly, patting it on the head.

Joe looked at Frank and couldn't help cracking a tiny smile. The huge dog couldn't really be named Bunny!

"Who do you three idiots think you are?" the girl yelled. "And"—she glared at Joe—"why do you have my invention in your hands?"

Joe looked down at the strange belt in his hand. "We were—"

She reached past the dog and grabbed the belt.

"Give me that! Did you think you could get away with this?" she demanded angrily.

"Excuse me, miss. Is there a problem?" a voice said from behind the group.

Joe and Frank watched as the girl spun around. A balding security guard, followed by several curious student inventors, stood in the aisle looking amused. The guard's smile faded when the dog turned around and growled deeply at him.

Frank said tensely, "Yeah, there's a problem. She won't call off her attack dog."

"Wait just a minute!" the girl snapped. "You were in my booth. Your blond friend had my leash in his hands." She turned back toward the guard. "They were terrorizing my dog with that robot," she said, pointing to Roger the Lobber, which was spinning its wheels against the fallen table.

"Hey, back off. If you'd calm down for a minute, we can tell you exactly what we were doing," Joe said angrily.

The guard grunted. "You." He pointed to the girl. "Call off that beast and—"

"He's not a beast!" she cried.

"*And,* as I was saying, all of you can follow me. We'll just take this matter to Mr. Zorba."

"Great introduction to our neighbor, Megan Sweetwater," Joe muttered under his breath.

"How about 'Not So Sweetwater,'" Frank whispered back.

After a moment Megan swung her shoulder-

13

length hair. "Bunny!" she ordered. "Over there. Bunny, now!" She pointed to the pile of clothing in the back of the booth. The dog walked around the table, giving the robot as wide a berth as possible. Bunny looked at everyone a little sadly, then plopped down on the sweatshirt.

"Miss, you have to tie up your dog. You can't just leave him loose," the guard said.

Megan frowned. "He hates being tied up. Did you see how well he obeys? He doesn't need to be tied." The dog began to growl when he heard his owner's voice getting more shrill.

"Tie him up," the guard said firmly.

After a lot of sighs and grumbles, Megan tied up her dog. She wrapped the nylon belt around her waist as Frank and Phil picked up the table and moved Roger to their own booth across the aisle.

The guard led the group down a flight of stairs to some classrooms that were being used as TIC committee offices.

"Okay, kids," the guard said. "The officials are just finishing up a meeting. Sit here until Mr. Zorba can see you." He gestured to a row of plastic chairs in an area of the hall set off by screens. While he was talking to the man at the reception desk, one of the classroom doors opened and a group of people walked out.

"Must be the judges. They sure look like a corporate bunch, with their blue and gray suits and their briefcases," Phil commented.

14

"Not all of them," Joe whispered, glancing at a pretty woman toward the back of the crowd. "She can't be much older than we are. I wonder how she fits into that group."

The woman's green fitted suit contrasted with her short auburn hair. The guys watched her leave the room.

"Hey, I know where I've seen her before," Frank said suddenly. "She's Tanya Zane, last year's competition winner. Each year the previous winner gets to be a judge. It's kind of an honorary position."

"I read about her in the program," Joe put in. "She invented a solar-powered jet ski. It's supposed to be coming out on the market next summer. She also got an internship with some big electronics company last summer."

"She also got a scholarship to Cal Tech," Frank added.

Phil whistled. "That's one of the most prestigious engineering schools in the country."

Before they could say more, a tall, athletic-looking blond man in his forties came up to them.

"I'm Nicholas Makowski, the competition's cochair," he said. "Back again, Megan? Let me assure you, your problem is getting top priority."

Megan didn't smile. "I hope so," she said flatly, "but now I've got a new one." She stabbed a finger at the Hardys and Phil. "Those three guys tried to steal my invention." She crossed her arms and frowned. "What are you going to do about it?"

Makowski looked taken aback. "Hold on there. That's a serious accusation," he said. "We'd better wait for Ari Zorba, my cochair. Come with me into the conference room."

Two minutes later, a gray-haired man of about fifty came into the room. He introduced himself as Ari Zorba and joined the group at the conference table.

"Don't tell me there is trouble already. A third of the inventors haven't even arrived yet," Zorba muttered, shaking his head. "In the last few expos," he growled, "we've been having way too many pranks.

He placed his hands firmly on the tabletop. Then he leaned forward and stared at the group. "All right, what's the problem here? Who's going to start?"

The teenagers looked at each other. Then Megan took a breath and began her accusation. "I had just gone to get something to drink. I took Bunny, my dog, because he hates being left alone. On the way back I stopped to talk to a friend on the aisle. When I looked down, Bunny was gone. Then I heard a yelp. I ran down the aisle. These three guys had knocked over my table on top of my dog and were tormenting it with their robot. The blond one had my invention, the radio-control leash, in his hands."

16

Megan held up the odd-looking belt. "He was going to steal it."

"Wait a minute!" Joe said hotly.

Frank nudged Joe to keep quiet, then started to explain. "Our robot's ball was missing. When we activated the robot to find the ball, it rolled straight into Megan's booth. The ball was under an old sweatshirt that was covered with dog hairs. My bet, Megan, is that your dog stole our ball."

Megan scowled and said, "Well, why was that guy there about to take my leash?"

Joe jumped in. "I wasn't about to take your leash. I just saw it and wondered what it was. I'm sorry if we upset you, but I hardly think you have any evidence of attempted theft."

"Anyway," Phil added, "if you had your dog with you, why didn't you control the monster with the radio-control leash?"

Megan's eyes flashed. "Monster? You and your friends are the monsters. The reason I didn't use my invention is that Bunny is so well trained that he no longer needs the leash. I didn't expect to find thieves in my booth when I returned only minutes later. Especially when the leash was well hidden."

"Enough!" Mr. Zorba exclaimed. "Megan, is there anything wrong with your leash?"

Megan examined it and shook her head. "Not that I can see. Something could have been altered in the components, but I wouldn't be able to tell until later."

"Well, there's not enough evidence against these boys to take action, at least now," Zorba said. Makowski nodded in agreement.

Zorba went on. "Boys, I'm warning you. Keep your hands on your own inventions. The penalty for theft is expulsion, and the law will be called in if necessary. You can leave now."

"But—" Joe burst out angrily. Frank kicked his brother under the table.

Makowski stood by the door as they were leaving. "Hope to see you all at the welcoming ceremonies on board tonight," he said as they passed by him. In a low voice, he added, "Sorry about all this. Ari can be pretty, uh, blunt."

"No kidding," Joe muttered.

"Thanks to you jokers, my poor dog is probably starving," Megan announced. "He should have been fed an hour ago." She stomped off toward the gym.

Joe glared at her back. "What's her beef?"

Frank shook his head. "She's a hothead, that's for sure. Let's give her a chance to clear out before we go back to the booth."

As they slowly walked up the stairs, Phil complained, "That guy Zorba didn't even listen to our side. Megan was accusing us unjustly, and he wouldn't let us defend ourselves."

"Yeah, he totally brushed us off. He looked so annoyed, you knew he wasn't listening to anything we were saying," Joe agreed.

Frank shrugged. "It's late. He probably wanted

to leave. Even if he didn't try to find out the truth, at least he didn't bust us."

"He had nothing on us," Joe said dryly. "Otherwise I'm sure he would have."

When they reached the gymnasium doors, they were closed. Joe stared at them, then down at his watch. "Six-ten," he said. "Guess what, guys. We're locked out."

"Great!" Frank gritted his teeth. "All our bags are inside. Man, this has been some day!"

After trying the locked doors one more time, the three boys left the building. Shivering in the frosty air, they followed the sidewalk around to the front, where the gym opened out onto the street. A security guard was locking the streetside doors.

"Wait!" Phil called out.

"Sir, we need to get in," Frank yelled as they sprinted up to the large oak doors.

"What's that?" the guard said. He turned and frowned when he recognized the Hardys. "What do you want now? You can't get in there. You knew when it was going to close."

"Please. Our luggage is in there. We came straight from O'Hare airport because our flight ran late," Frank explained.

The guard eyed the three guys. Then, grumbling, he put the key back into the lock.

"Don't ask me for any more favors," he growled. He threw the door open and flipped a switch. Light flooded the deserted gymnasium.

Frank followed Phil and Joe through the aisles. "Doesn't it seem as if there are fewer inventions than there were earlier?" he called.

When nobody answered, he looked up to see Phil and Joe frozen in front of their booth.

Frank stepped up to the booth.

"Roger!" he gasped. "Someone took our robot!"

3 Windy City Plunge

Frank slammed his fist on the table. "You know why so many inventions are gone? Because people are scared to leave them here overnight— they get stolen," he said bitterly.

His brown eyes smoldered as he surveyed the booth. The Hardys' duffel bag and Phil's backpack were in the corner where they had left them. When Frank stepped over to the duffel and picked it up, the orange tennis ball rolled up against the booth divider. "Some good that does us," he muttered.

Joe slid Roger's carrying case out from under the table and opened it. A single bolt fell to the floor.

Phil gasped. "Man, they even took my tools! I can't believe this!"

Frank and Joe took off down the aisle. Hoping the thief might have hidden the robot in another booth, the two brothers split up and made a quick search through the rest of the gym.

As Joe was checking the aisles close to the street entrance, he saw a head pop around the door. A curly-haired guy in a black wool coat peered in and smiled.

"So you're the ones the guard was grumbling about," he said. "I'm Byron Paige. I had just left when I saw the lights go on. The gym was supposed to close fifteen minutes ago, wasn't it? Is something up?"

Joe ran his hand through his hair distractedly. "Yeah, I'll tell you what's up. Someone stole our invention."

"You're kidding," Byron said, frowning. "That's rough. I'd be furious if someone took my stationery maker. What's your invention?"

"A robot that retrieves tennis balls and shoots them back. I just don't know how someone could walk off with a four-foot-high robot," Joe muttered.

Byron rubbed his hands together to warm them. A big greenish stone on his silver ring caught the light. "You know, I'd like to give you a hand, but I'm already running late for dinner with my parents. They'd have a cow if I didn't show up. They're leaving town later tonight. But I know a lot of kids at the competition. I'll start getting the word out."

22

Joe nodded as Byron took off down the steps. Back at the booth, one look at his brother's tense face told Joe that Frank had fared no better.

Joe kicked the wall. "I'll bet you anything it was Megan. She was really mad at us. Plus, she probably had the whole gym to herself when she came back to get that mutt of hers." He strode across the aisle into Megan's booth. A wrinkled TIC program was the only sign that she had been there earlier.

"We aren't exactly her best friends, but then again, anyone could have stolen Roger while we were in the office," Frank said grimly.

His brother shook his head. "But why?"

Phil pushed his hair out of his eyes. "Do you think someone wants to win so much that whoever it is would steal other people's inventions? I mean, Roger *is* pretty cool. It could win."

"We need to tell the guard. He might have seen something," Frank said.

"Tell me what?" said a gruff voice. Frowning, the guard was walking toward the boys.

"Our invention was stolen," Phil said.

"Don't look at us like we're crazy," Joe said between clenched teeth. "You didn't see someone leaving with five-foot-tall robot that answers to the name of Roger, did you?"

"Nope," the guard said. "Sorry," he added, not sounding terribly sincere.

Frank stepped forward. "Well, who do we report this to?"

23

"Me," the man answered. "But there's nothing I can do until morning. Tomorrow I'll file the proper reports. Security will be on the lookout."

"On the lookout?" Joe yelled. "What about the competition? My brother and his partner don't have an invention anymore."

"You'll have to talk to Mr. Makowski or Mr. Zorba. They deal with the rules. Right now, I'm closing up. Let's go," the guard said over his shoulder as he walked toward the door.

The boys grabbed their bags and trudged out onto the street. They turned south on Canal Street and walked the ten minutes to the hotel where the competitors were staying.

"That guard was a real jerk," Phil complained as they walked through the lobby doors. "What's wrong with everyone here?"

Frank shook his head. "Beats me. Look, let's grab some dinner," he suggested. "We'll meet up with the group in the lobby at seven-thirty to go to the welcoming ceremonies. It'll be a good chance to talk to Megan and anyone else who might know where Roger is."

After a quick meal in the hotel restaurant, the guys returned to their sixth-floor room to shower and change. Phil told the Hardys to go on ahead so he could call home. With all the excitement, he'd forgotten his promise to phone once he'd arrived. They made plans to hook up with Phil in the lobby and then headed to the elevator. The old-fashioned car bumped to a stop, and the grate

24

squeaked open. The boys joined a noisy group of student inventors already in the car.

"Do you think Makowski will help Zorba out any?" a voice in the elevator said as it started down.

"I hope so. There were too many problems last year for Zorba to handle by himself," a deep voice answered. "Remember all those pranks? It's good they gave him a cochair this year."

A tall, freckled girl in the back chimed in, "Zorba doesn't think it's good. I heard he's insulted—he's a professional conference coordinator, and Makowski's just an engineer. But I'm glad Makowski's working with him. Maybe Makowski will loosen up the old grump a bit."

"We should put on a musical about ol' Ari," someone else said. "Zorba the Grouch."

Just then the elevator reached the lobby. Joe nudged Frank. "Megan's over by the window," he said quietly. "Dark hair, red coat."

Both Hardys started toward her. But just then, Megan turned and spotted them. She spun around quickly and started pushing past people toward the back of the lobby.

"Wait, Megan," Joe called. "Could we talk to you for a minute?"

Megan set her mouth in a hard, thin line. Before Joe could close the gap between them, she made an abrupt turn, right into the ladies' room.

"Great," Frank muttered. "We'll get her later."

"Get who later? Megan?" a voice said from the side. The Hardys whirled around. A tall teenager in a black coat was leaning against the wall.

"Byron," Joe said. "I thought you were eating with your parents."

"Didn't last long. We did the diner thing," Byron said casually.

Joe introduced Frank and explained how he and Byron had met earlier at the gymnasium.

"Did you guys find your robot?" Byron asked.

Frank shook his head. "No such luck. Listen, we've got to find our friend," he said, not really in the mood to talk.

Byron didn't take the hint. He tagged along behind the brothers. They found Phil standing by the dining room door. He pointed to a young woman with short auburn hair who was sitting at a table with a muscular guy with spiky black hair.

"Isn't that Tanya Zane?" Phil asked Frank.

"That's her, all right," Byron said before Frank could answer. "And the guy with her is Yueh Chu. He's an inventor from her high school. Rumor has it they were good friends in school. Rumor also has it she's not exactly going to be impartial in her judging."

"There seem to be a lot of rumors flying around, considering we've only been here for half a day," Frank observed. "How does everyone know so much about one another?"

"A lot of us were competitors last year," Byron explained. "Also, a lot of us do other smaller competitions outside of TIC." He looked up as someone called his name. "Hey, gotta go. There are some of my buddies waving to me."

A honk sounded from outside, signaling that the shuttle bus to the cruise had arrived. The three friends got in line for seats.

On the bus, Frank leaned over to Joe and whispered, "Megan still hadn't come out of the bathroom by the time we left the lobby. I wonder if she'll make it to the cruise."

"She sure is acting strange," Joe said.

Phil wiped the steam off the bus window. "Everything's been strange at this competition," he said gloomily. "But if we don't get Roger back before tomorrow morning at ten, there won't *be* any competition for us."

Twenty minutes later, the group of inventors got out at Chicago's Navy Pier on Lake Michigan and started boarding the cruise ship.

The loudspeaker crackled into the crisp air as the last of the group boarded the ship. "Good evening, everyone. My name is Captain Quadly. On behalf of the *Windy City Princess*, we would like to welcome you to Chicago.

"For the first part of the cruise, we'll have a band on the lower level. Fortunately, the weather has cleared up. So, on the upper deck, we'll be offering a tour of Chicago sights. We leave in five minutes. Enjoy your trip."

The guys headed up a carpeted flight of stairs. At the top, large swinging doors opened onto the deck. In front of them, a crowd of young inventors were checking out the ship.

A woman stood by the doors. To her right, the deck narrowed into a corridor that led to the ship's stern. In the dim light, Frank saw a set of ladderlike steps that led to a small observation platform.

The table beside the woman was piled high with what looked like quilted red-and-blue flannel shirts. She smiled at Phil and the Hardys. "Would you boys care for a Thermo-Coat?" she asked. "One of you student inventors came up with it two years ago. See this dial here?" She pointed to a small plastic disk at the base of a coat. "You turn it to control the amount of warmth you want."

Phil examined the coat. "Cool! Hey, I'll take one," he said. The woman handed him a coat. Frank reached out and grabbed one, too.

"I don't need one," Joe said. He puffed his chest out. "I can take it."

Frank nudged Phil and said, "My brother's a real man." Then he pulled the oversize coat over the jacket he was wearing and led the way to the rail, where the guys watched the boat pull away from the dock.

The audio tour began with the story of the cow who kicked over a lantern and started the fire that burned down the city of Chicago in 1871. About halfway through the story, Frank heard a strange clicking noise beside him. He looked over.

It was Joe. His teeth were chattering violently. Frank started to laugh. "Get yourself a coat, macho man," he said.

Joe threw him a dirty look, got up, and returned with his own Thermo-Coat.

"I looked for Megan while I was up," Joe reported in a low voice. "Couldn't find her."

At the end of the tour, everyone went down to the lower level for dessert. The Hardys sat down at a five-person table and saved a seat for Phil, who was getting dessert. A pretty girl with beads braided into her hair was already seated.

"Hi. You're the guys who spooked Megan's dog, aren't you?" she asked. "My name is Kara Melia."

"Yeah. I'm Frank, and this is my brother, Joe. My inventing partner, Phil, is over at the counter. How did you know who we were?" Frank asked.

Kara tilted her head. "Oh, word gets around. Byron told me about you, as a matter of fact. He's the gossip king—he knows everything about everyone."

Phil came back from the buffet with a slice of cake and slid into his seat. He poked Frank under the table and nodded toward the far side of the room. "Megan's at the table behind the piano with a bunch of other girls," he whispered.

All of a sudden, the kids at a nearby table burst

out laughing. Phil raised his eyebrows. "Maybe we're sitting at the wrong table."

Frank craned his neck toward the table and said, "Look at the guy who's holding his hand upside down and shaking it. He's turning red."

"There's Byron on his right," Phil said. "He's cracking up. Hey, I think it's his ring that's causing that guy so much trouble. Must be a gag ring that squeezes the victim's finger."

"Byron's got hold of the kid's hand. There, the ring's off. What a joker!" Frank exclaimed.

"No kidding," Kara said, frowning. "He just can't turn down a chance to get attention."

Before anyone could respond, a woman got up and announced that the welcoming ceremony would start on the upper deck. Kara excused herself and took off to find some friends.

"Let's try to catch Megan," Joe said. By the time the boys crossed the room, however, Megan was nowhere to be seen.

"All right," Frank said firmly, "when you get up to the deck, grab seats in the last row. We *are* going to talk to her after the program."

Phil led the Hardys to the crowd at the bottom of the stairs. After waiting for several minutes, they made it out to the deck. The boys stumbled over the seated people until they reached the only spots left in the back row.

"Man," Frank sighed, "I can't see a thing. It doesn't help that the lighting's so dim." He leaned forward, trying to spot Megan in the mass of heads in front of him.

All of a sudden, the lights surrounding the podium flashed on. Pink haze streamed from the four lamps aimed at the speaker. The reflections in the lake made strange pink ripples that glowed through the bars on the rail.

"Heat lamps," Phil whispered. "They're brand-new and superefficient. I read about them in one of my science magazines."

Ari Zorba walked to the podium. His gray hair looked pink under the lights. He began to speak. But Frank stopped listening when he spotted a girl with shoulder-length dark hair in one of the aisle seats on the right. He squinted, trying to get a better look. "Is that Megan?" he asked Joe.

Joe looked, then nodded. On the podium, Zorba was introducing Nicholas Makowski.

As Makowski started his speech, Megan stood up and walked toward the stairs.

Joe turned to his brother and raised his eyebrow. Frank looked at the row of people they'd have to climb over to follow her. He shook his head.

"We'll catch her after the talk. We're on a ship—she can't escape," Frank whispered.

The Hardys turned their attention back to the speaker. "Nothing is more important than a good rapport between the best minds of today's youth and the foremost adult innovators of our nation," Makowski was saying. "I'd like to—"

31

Makowski suddenly stopped speaking. A look of horror came over his face, and he jerked to the side. From somewhere behind the audience there was a faint whooshing noise.

As the startled man leapt to the side, his foot slid off the top step of the platform. His arms flailed wildly as he tried to regain his balance.

"He's going over!" someone screamed as Makowski swayed dangerously close to the rail.

Frank jumped to his feet. But before he could move, Makowski plunged over the iron bar into the icy December water.

4 Rockin' Rocket

"He'll freeze to death if someone doesn't get to him immediately!" Frank yelled as he leapt over some fallen chairs. The Hardys plowed their way through a group of anxious inventors.

"He's drowning!" a plump boy shouted.

"Where is he? I don't see him," another voice yelled into the frosty air.

Frank turned to Zorba, who was wringing his hands. "Get the emergency crew!" Frank ordered.

Joe ripped one of the heat lamps off its post and held it over the water. In the pink haze he could just make out Makowski's still form.

"There he is!" Joe cried, dropping the light to the deck. Taking off his coat, he ran up the steps

33

to the platform and dived over the rail into the icy water.

Joe felt his hands slice through the surface. As the frigid water hit the rest of his body, his chest tightened—he could barely breathe!

He struggled to clear the sudden heaviness from his mind. Which way was it to the top?

Frantically, he kicked his legs. His lungs were exploding. Then something hit the water near his head. Joe tried to swim toward the sound.

Frank anxiously watched the flotation device he had thrown overboard. The only sign of his brother was a ring of choppy waves coming from the spot where he had gone under.

Then his blond head bobbed up. "To your left, Joe!" Frank yelled.

Joe paddled to his left, reaching for the orange float. Frank sighed in relief as Joe pulled it to his chest. Makowski was floating on his stomach a couple feet away. As soon as Joe was secure, he reached out with his free arm and grabbed the unconscious man's collar.

"Above you, kid! Sling coming down," a voice yelled from the deck. When Joe looked up, he was blinded by a bright spotlight.

Trying to gain his bearings, Joe was glad to hear his brother's voice. "Put Makowski in the sling. Then grab the ladder," Frank directed, as he lowered a rope ladder.

Joe let the flotation device go. Treading water,

he grabbed the sling and secured the wide strip of rubber under Makowski's limp body.

When the crew saw Joe give the thumbs-up, they started to haul Makowski up to the deck.

"You're doing fine," Frank yelled. He watched his brother reach for the ladder. Slowly, Joe pulled himself up the side.

Frank grabbed Joe's arm and helped him over the railing. The emergency crew cheered as he stumbled onto the deck.

"Are you okay?" Frank asked as he wrapped a blanket around Joe's shoulders.

Joe nodded. "How's Makowski?" he asked through chattering teeth.

Frank looked inquiringly at the ship's doctor, who had just come up to the brothers.

"He'll be okay," the doctor told Joe. "He's lucky, let me tell you. He was seconds away from succumbing to hypothermia." The doctor clapped Joe on the shoulder. "If it hadn't been for your quick thinking, we might've lost him. Now, let's get you downstairs and check you out."

Frank grabbed one of Joe's arms, and Phil took the other. Together, they followed the young doctor to the stairs.

The ship was heading back to the dock now. The teen inventors were scheduled to go to a special reception at the Museum of Science and Industry. Joe leaned over to Frank and whispered in his ear, "Before we get off, see if you can find out what happened."

Frank stared at him with worried brown eyes. Joe assured him, "It's all right. I'm fine."

Frank nodded. His brother had been in so many scrapes, he knew his own limits.

As Frank went back up, the coldness pressed in on him as he stepped onto the deserted deck.

Climbing the steps to the podium, he looked around. Something had startled Makowski right before he went over. Whatever it was, it must have been on the small observation platform, Frank quickly decided.

He walked past the swinging doors, past the table with the Thermo-Coats, and turned down the corridor between the railing and the wall. In the shadows toward the boat's stern, he groped for the ladderlike staircase he'd seen earlier.

His hand touched cold, damp metal. He pulled himself up the slippery rungs cautiously. On the top step, he surveyed the small deck. A solid, waist-high wall surrounded the platform, except for where the stairs came up.

He faced the podium. If someone had stood up here, they would have been visible to Makowski. Was that what had startled him so?

Frank played back the scene in his mind. Wait! Right before Makowski had gone over, there had been a faint whooshing noise. Like something flying through the air. Could somebody have thrown something at Makowski from above?

Frank got to his knees and groped along the concrete, hunting for anything an attacker might have dropped as he fled. But he found nothing.

He stood up with a sigh and started down the narrow steps, back first. As he was lowering his foot onto the second rung, though, his top foot slipped from under him. He was falling!

"Whoa!" he shouted. He grabbed the top step with his hand. Dangling by one arm from the ladder, he reached up to the platform wall. But he couldn't get a good grip. As his hand slipped downward, his fingers hit a ledge. Grabbing hard, he managed to steady himself and pull his legs securely back onto the steps.

As he pulled his hand out, the tips of his fingers hit something sitting on the ledge. He pulled out a heavy cylindrical object.

"Can't see a thing in this light," Frank muttered. He slid the object into his jacket and made his way back down to the deck. Stopping under the lights by the doors to the lower level, he pulled out the curious object.

So that's why it didn't roll off the ledge, Frank thought. The thing wasn't a true cylinder—it had twelve sides. It looked like a big flashlight with a hole the size of a golf ball in one end. Could it be a launcher of some kind?

He pushed the button on the outside. When

nothing happened, he peered down the hole. There were several coarse brown hairs in the barrel. Frank pursed his lips. Those hairs looked as if they might have come from Megan's dog.

Putting the object back under his coat, Frank went up to the podium. Not really knowing what he was looking for, he stepped up to the rail.

The ship was pulling close to the lighted dock. As Frank turned away, out of the corner of his eye he saw a gleam from a coil of rope hanging on a hook. Curious, he reached into the coils—and pulled out a stubby arrow.

Frank whistled. Then he stuck the weapon into his jacket pocket and went to find his brother and Phil.

They were lined up to get off the boat. Joe still had on his wet corduroys, but he had swapped his jacket and sweater for a Thermo-Coat. "So did you find anything?" he asked impatiently.

The ship docked, and the gangplank was lowered. "Plenty," Frank said in a low voice. "Has Makowski said anything about how it happened?"

Phil shrugged. "He just says he lost his balance and fell. It was an accident. Why?"

"It was no accident," Frank replied.

"What?" Joe exclaimed as the line started to move. "How do you know?"

"I found an arrow that someone shot at him."

"Who? Why?" Phil interjected.

"That's what we need to learn," Frank said.

"What's our plan?" Joe asked eagerly.

"Phil and I will go to the reception and snoop around. You should go back to the hotel and get a good night's rest," Frank told his brother. "Look." He pointed toward the parking lot, where the ship's medic was beckoning Joe toward a taxi. Makowski had just gotten into another cab and driven off. "Your car is waiting, sir."

"Cut it out, Frank," Joe grumbled. "I'm fine! I'll go back to the hotel and change, and then I'll meet you at the museum."

Frank grinned. "Now, how did I know that's what you'd say?"

Joe headed for the cab. Phil dug his hands into his pockets and shivered. "I'm freezing. When do the buses come?" he said.

Frank shrugged absently. He was scanning the crowd of inventors. "Megan has vanished again," he muttered. "Do you see her anywhere?"

"Maybe she took a taxi," Phil suggested. "She seems like a loner. Maybe she didn't feel like taking the bus with everyone else."

Just then, the buses rolled into the parking lot. Frank looked at his friend and shook his head. "I wonder . . . Come on, let's get a seat. I'll show you what I found tonight."

The guys found seats at the back, away from everyone else. Once they were moving, Frank took out a penlight. Then he pulled the black cylinder out from his jacket and handed it to Phil.

"Wow," Phil exclaimed as he turned the object over in his hand. "What is it?"

Silently, Frank reached into his pocket and handed Phil the dartlike arrow. The red paint on its tip was flaking off. The stem was clear, hard Lucite that ended in three small feathery projections made of flexible red plastic.

Phil frowned. "The arrow fits into this?" he asked, as he started to slide the arrow into the black plastic barrel.

"Wait," Frank cautioned. He took the black thing from Phil and pointed the penlight down the hole. "See those brown hairs?"

Phil leaned over to look. "They look like dog hairs—hey! You think they're from Megan's dog?" he whispered.

"Could be," Frank answered. "We'll have to check that out later. This arrow is definitely the thing that startled Makowski."

"But—" Phil paused to think. "Why would Megan shoot at Makowski? And why would he say it was just an accident?" he asked.

"Don't know. He may not have actually seen anything—all he knows is something startled him, and maybe she was ticked about his refusal to punish us for supposedly taking her leash. But we can't be sure she's involved," Frank said. He slid the arrow down the hole. A quarter of it stuck out of the barrel. The hole was too wide to hold the arrow steady.

Phil reached over Frank's arm, grabbed the clear stem, and pressed the arrow as far back as possible. All of a sudden there was a click. The arrow fit securely into the barrel, with just the tip sticking out.

"It's to shoot the arrow, all right," Phil said. "That button is the trigger."

"Yup. We'll try it out in our room to see how it works. I was thinking . . . it might be a TIC invention," Frank said.

"It wouldn't be that difficult to make. But it's against TIC rules to enter weapons in the competition," Phil pointed out.

Just then the bus came to a stop in the museum parking lot. Frank rewrapped the arrow and launcher in his jacket, and the two boys followed the other inventors inside.

Near the door, the boys found a group of kids looking at a showcase on comets. Byron Paige was standing next to it, lecturing.

"Think about it. If Comet Swift-Tuttle had hit the earth in 1992," he said, "everyone would be dead now. The planet would have burst into flames. Life as we know it would be over."

"Cool," a short guy with glasses said.

The girl on his right rolled her eyes. "You're sick," she said. "Hey, Byron, where did Comet Swift-Tuttle come from?"

"Well," Byron said grandly, "there's a blizzard

41

of comets out by Mercury in this thing called the Ert Cloud. . . ."

Frank cleared his throat. "Uh, Byron? That's Oort Cloud, not Ert Cloud. And it's beyond Pluto, not Mercury."

Phil couldn't keep from chuckling. The other teenagers watched Byron in expectant silence.

Byron glared at Frank. He spun on his heel and started walking away. "You guys believe who you want," he said over his shoulder.

Frank shrugged, trying not to grin, and he and Phil moved away. Phil stopped to check out a case of asteroid fragments. Frank wandered on.

Toward the back of the room, there was a big roped-off model of the Russian *Energia* rocket. The model, on a stand, was about ten feet tall, not nearly as big as the original.

As Frank neared the rocket, he heard a muffled tapping coming from inside. He knew he wasn't imagining things when Kara, the girl the boys had met on the cruise, looked over, too.

Seeing Frank, she pointed to the rocket. "Did you hear that? Weird," she said as she walked toward the ropes to get a better look.

Frank followed her. As they got closer, the tapping got louder. People nearby turned their heads in surprise.

Thump. Thump. Thump. Thump.

All of a sudden, the rocket started wobbling on its base. The heavy model tipped forward.

"Kara! Look out! It's going to fall!" Frank yelled. He sprang toward her as the rocket hung in the air, teetering on its base.

He slammed into Kara's back, pushing her as far to the side as he could. He felt himself falling. His chest hit the carpet.

Then the rocket landed with a heavy thud— right on top of him.

5 Cabbie Confessions

Joe had just walked into the room when he heard a crash. He looked over and saw his brother lying pinned under the huge model rocket.

"Frank!" Joe sprinted over and knelt beside his brother. He tried to heave the model off Frank's back, but it was too heavy. "Someone help me!" he yelled. Then, looking up, he saw Phil's worried face.

"Phil! Grab the other side. I'll push, you pull," Joe ordered.

The guys slowly moved the rocket to the side.

Frank moaned, and struggled to a sitting position. "Uggh! I'm okay—just a little bruised. Get that rocket open, Joe."

For the first time, Joe noticed the desperate pounding coming from inside the model.

As Joe struggled with the rocket door, Phil helped Frank to his feet. "Lucky for you this rocket has a wide base. If that hadn't hit the ground first and stopped the rocket from landing flat on the floor, you'd have been squashed," he said. His tone was light, but Frank saw that his hands were shaking.

The two friends stepped over to the rocket, where Joe was using his penknife to pry open the door. Anxiously, he flipped it open. The teenagers who had gathered around gasped as Megan Sweetwater, tied and gagged, fell out onto the carpet.

Frank's dark eyes widened. He bent over Megan's crumpled figure. She was blinking furiously to keep the tears from spilling over.

"Megan, are you all right?" Frank asked gently, as he removed her gag. Joe and Phil untied her arms and legs. All the frightened girl could do was take long, deep breaths to keep from crying.

"What's going on here? Make room. What's going on?" a gruff voice called. Ari Zorba pushed his way through the crowd. When Frank started toward him, Zorba groaned. "You again! You attract trouble. What's—"

The gray-haired man stopped grumbling when he saw the fallen rocket and a tearful Megan sitting on the ground. "Oh my," he gasped. "What happened?"

While Frank briefed him, a security guard

made his way through the crowd. Together, the two men listened to Frank's story.

"Okay, thanks. You boys run along," Mr. Zorba said tiredly. "I'll handle this now."

Frank bristled. "Wait—" he started to say. But Zorba had turned his back on him and was talking intently to the guard.

The guard nodded and started to break up the crowd. A moment later Zorba took Megan by the arm and led her to a door across the room.

"What a jerk!" Joe fumed as he and Phil joined Frank. "He wouldn't even let us talk to Megan."

"The way our luck's been going, we'll *never* get to talk to her," Phil grumbled. "We've been after her all evening."

The boys looked around at the empty room. All the other teenagers had gone into the Omnimax theater to watch a film.

"Let's wait here for Megan. She'll probably want to go back to the hotel when she gets done talking to Zorba," Frank said.

Phil and Joe nodded. "We can check out the area, too," Joe added. "Maybe we'll find some trace of Megan's attacker."

But the search turned up nothing. Finally the door Zorba and Megan had gone through opened. Megan walked out alone, a heavy frown on her face.

It softened when she caught sight of the guys. "Oh," she said, sounding surprised. She touched Frank's arm. "I owe you one. Thanks."

"How are you feeling?" Phil asked.

She crinkled her forehead. "Okay, I guess. My brain hurts more than anything else."

"Do you want to go back to the hotel? If you want, we'll get a cab with you," Frank offered.

"That'd be good," she answered gratefully.

As they walked toward the door, Frank asked her if she knew what had happened.

Her frown returned and she clenched her fists. "When we got off the ship, I grabbed a cab and came here early. I really wanted to see this exhibit, but I didn't feel like dealing with all those people. It's been a—a bad day. I was just going to check out the exhibit, then leave.

"Anyway, when I got here the place was deserted. I was just looking around when someone suddenly grabbed me from behind. He jammed his hand to my mouth so I couldn't scream. I bit the guy's hand, but then he put a cloth over my face. Next thing I knew, I woke up in that terrible rocket model."

"A cloth?" Joe repeated. He held the door open and the teenagers trooped outside to the street. "What did it smell like?"

Megan wrinkled her nose. "Horrible. Sweet."

"Must have been chloroform," Frank said.

Phil flagged down a cab. After everyone was seated, Megan cleared her throat. "I guess I should say, well, I'm sorry."

She met Joe's eyes, and added, "I'm sorry for

accusing you of trying to steal my leash and for calling all of you some pretty awful names."

Joe grinned. "Apology accepted. Now tell us what's going on. Why would anyone want to knock you out and stuff you into a model rocket?"

Megan laughed shakily. "It sounds so ridiculous, doesn't it?" Then her face sobered. "It's a long story, and I don't know how much of it I really understand but . . . A couple of days before the competition in New Mexico, I got a typed letter asking me to sell my radio leash for fifteen thousand dollars."

"Fifteen thousand dollars! Wow!" Phil exclaimed from the front seat.

"Who sent the letter?" Frank questioned.

"The letterhead just had a company name, Preton, Inc. There was no return address," Megan replied. "Anyway, the letter said a company representative would call to make the arrangements. Well, the money was tempting, but if I win the TIC competition, I get a four-year scholarship to any university, which is worth a whole lot more than fifteen thousand dollars. Plus, these TIC conventions give us the best opportunities to get summer internships with the top companies."

"Good point," Phil said. His tone was full of admiration.

Before Megan could go on, the taxi pulled up to the hotel. The teenagers paid and went into the hotel restaurant to have some hot chocolate and finish talking.

"Go on, Megan. You were talking about the people that wanted to buy your leash," Frank said.

Megan nodded. "A man did call the next night and said he was from Preton, Inc. When I refused his offer, he got all unfriendly and hung up."

"Wait," Joe interrupted. "How could he have known about the leash? Were you in the news or anything?"

Frank leaned forward intently. It was a good question. If Megan's invention wasn't public knowledge, it would narrow down the suspects a lot.

But Megan was nodding. "My hometown paper did a feature story on me. It's a small town, and they get pretty excited when one of the residents gets an award or anything like that. Still, it's a very small paper. I can't believe anyone outside of Hobbs would have seen it."

"It's possible, though," Frank said, sighing.

"Anyway," Megan went on, "nothing happened until I got to Chicago this morning."

"Then what?" Phil asked, staring at her.

"When I got into the hotel," she explained, "there was an unsigned note at the front desk for me. It said 'Accidents have a way of happening to uncooperative people.'"

"Was it typed?" Joe asked.

"Yes," she confirmed. "On plain white paper. I threw it out. Anyway, a woman from Preton called soon after and offered to buy the leash

49

again. And again, I refused. But by then I was getting scared. I mean, with all those phone calls and a threatening note . . ."

"Of course," Phil said sympathetically.

"So I went to set up my booth at Cahill. That's when I ran into you guys and flipped out," Megan finished sheepishly.

"Hey, it's understandable. Let's forget it." Joe grinned.

"Thanks. Anyway, I went back to the hotel after that awful meeting with Zorba and Makowski. This morning I had talked to Makowski about the problems I was having. He said he'd talk to security. He told me not to worry, that everything would be okay. Well, tonight I got another phone call. A voice I didn't recognize said that he knew who was after me. I should meet him at eight forty-five during the welcoming cruise to find out more."

"So," Frank said, "that's why you left during Makowski's speech? Did you meet the caller on the observation platform?" He watched her closely as he said the words.

Megan gave him a puzzled look, which quickly hardened into a suspicious glare. "How did you know that I was supposed to meet him up there? You weren't the guy who called, were you?"

Frank shook his head somberly. "Someone shot at Makowski with an arrow. The arrow was shot off that top platform," he answered.

Megan crossed her arms. "Are you saying that *I* shot at Makowski?" she said coldly. "I didn't even get to the platform. The only way to get up was by this old, slippery ladder. I realized how dangerous it could be to go up there, considering what's been going on. I went down to the lower level to warm up and think about things."

"Did anyone see you?" Frank asked.

"No one else was there," Megan replied. Then her eyes widened as she understood what Frank's question meant. "Look, I only found out about Makowski falling into the lake when I heard the loudspeaker calling for the emergency crew. If you think I shot an arrow at him, you're crazy!"

Joe smiled. "Relax. Frank didn't mean that," he said, trying to calm her down. He shot his brother a glare. Wasn't it obvious to Frank that Megan had been framed?

Frank wasn't so sure. Megan's story sounded reasonable, but he'd known plenty of guilty people who sounded reasonable. He wasn't going to make up his mind one way or the other until he knew more.

Phil suddenly gave a huge yawn. "Sorry," he said. "I'm beat!"

"I'm with you, Phil. Totally wiped," Frank said, as he got up from the table.

"We'll walk you to your room, Megan," Joe offered. "Just to make sure no one's waiting there for you."

She smiled at him. "Thanks."

As they got on the elevator, Frank realized there was one matter they hadn't cleared up yet.

"By the way, Megan," he said casually, "how's your dog? I bet he was pretty lonely when you went to get him after our meeting with Makowski and Zorba. I mean, the gym must have been deserted by the time you got there."

Megan raised her eyebrow. "I didn't know you cared about my dog," she said as the group stepped into the elevator. "There were still a few people in the gym when I got back. You should have seen Bunny, though. He's *totally* afraid of your robot. When we walked by it, he just stuck his tail between his legs and whimpered. You really terrorized the poor guy," she joked.

The elevator bumped to a stop on Megan's floor. As they all got out and started walking toward Megan's room, Joe tapped his brother on the arm. Behind Phil's and Megan's backs, he silently mouthed the words "She didn't steal Roger."

"So you saw our robot?" Phil asked.

Megan looked at him strangely. "Right where you left the little electronic monster," she said. Then her face clouded up. "Why?" she said. "Is something wrong? Wasn't I supposed to see it?"

"It was gone when we got there," Phil said.

"And you thought I—?" Megan whirled to glare at Frank. "I can't believe you guys! You don't care about my dog," she said angrily. "You thought I stole your robot. You were just trying to trap me into saying I'd done it."

Frank sighed. This girl had a temper. "Look, Megan, I'm sorry. The robot disappeared about the time you went to get your dog. You were really upset with us. It didn't take a lot to think that you could have stolen our robot. We just want to get everything straightened out. If we don't get Roger back before tomorrow morning, we're out of the contest," he explained.

"Did you see anyone around our booth?" Joe asked earnestly.

Megan shook her head. "No," she said stiffly. She was clearly angry. "I just want you to know, I would never have taken your invention."

The four teens continued down the hall in uncomfortable silence.

When they rounded the corner, Megan gasped. "The light! My door—it's open. . . ." She broke into a run. The Hardys and Phil sprinted after her.

They caught up to her as she stepped into her room. Trembling, she leaned against the closet to steady herself. Frank and Joe pushed past her.

Sweaters, jeans, socks, and papers were strewn all over the carpet. The mattress was propped against the dresser.

The room had been ransacked!

6 Runaway Robot

"Let's make sure no one's still here," Joe whispered.

Megan didn't hear him. "My papers!" she cried as she scrambled to her night table. She yanked the drawer out and dumped it upside down on the bed. Taped to the underside was a brown packet. She heaved a sigh of relief.

"Anything but these," she said. "They're the specs for the leash. I'm so glad I stuck the actual leash in the hotel safe."

Frank and Joe, meanwhile, had checked out the bathroom and the closet to make sure the intruder wasn't still lurking.

"Better see if anything else is missing," Joe said.

While Megan looked over her belongings, Joe

and Phil walked over to the door and inspected the lock and saw it wasn't broken. "It must have been picked," Joe observed.

"We'll help pick up," Frank volunteered. He pointed to a crumpled heap of clothing. "I'll start putting these in some kind of order."

As he folded her sweatshirts into a stack, he carefully plucked a few of Bunny's hairs off Megan's clothes and dropped them between the pages of the TIC program he had in his pocket.

"Nothing's missing that I can see," Megan announced after a few minutes.

"Well, they didn't want your money," Frank said as Megan put an envelope of bills that had fallen from her suitcase into her jeans pocket. "If it's the leash they're after, why?"

Megan bit her lip. Sitting on the bed, she said, "I guess it could make a lot of money—I mean, lots of people have dogs."

"How does it work?" Phil wanted to know.

"It's a modification of the radio tracking collar that a lot of hunting dogs wear," Megan explained. "Only I programmed a chip that sends a signal to the dog when it gets beyond a given radius from whoever's wearing the belt."

"Very cool!" Phil said enthusiastically.

"Thanks." Megan looked anxious. "I planned to file for a patent after the contest is over, but now I'm wondering if I'll even have anything to file."

"You will if we can help it," Joe promised.

Megan's face was happier as she picked up the phone to call security.

In a few minutes, the night manager and a security guard knocked on the door. Extremely apologetic, the night manager insisted that Megan move to a new room and offered each of the teenagers a pair of gift certificates to a fancy restaurant down the street. As the Hardys and Phil left, Megan was giving the guard a statement and the manager was dialing the police station.

In their own room, Frank pulled the launcher and arrow from his jacket. He gave Joe the lowdown on what he and Phil had deduced about the weapon.

Then, using a pair of tweezers, Frank pulled a short brown hair out of the launcher. It matched the dog hairs he had taken from Megan's room. He put the samples in plastic bags.

"Someone could have planted those hairs," Joe said.

"Sure," Frank agreed.

"I think she's innocent," Phil burst out. "She didn't try to kill Makowski."

"I'm not saying she did," Frank said quietly. "I just want the facts to speak for themselves.

"Hey, look at this," he went on, staring down the hole. With the tweezers, he pointed to a small black rectangular panel stuck to the inside. It looked like a computer chip.

Phil peered in. "It's for a remote control. See how it's touching the trigger wires?"

"You mean the launcher could have been fired from a distance?" Joe said excitedly.

"Uh-huh. But not," Phil added hastily, "from as far away as the lower deck of the ship."

"But that means anyone could have done it," Joe pointed out. "We've got a lot of suspects!"

"Let's see this thing shoot," Frank said. He dug around in the desk for something to aim at. Pulling a Chicago phone book out of the top drawer, he held it up, away from his body.

"Here goes!" Phil aimed the weapon at the book and pressed the button on the outside.

The arrow shot out of the barrel and into the thick book, knocking it out of Frank's hand.

"Wow!" Joe exclaimed. He picked up the book. The head of the arrow was sticking out the far side. "That could kill a person."

Frank nodded grimly. "We need to ask Makowski who might want him dead. And, Phil, will you check into the launcher tomorrow? Try to find out if it has anything to do with the competition. It may be that it's a legitimate invention that was modified to be a weapon. Ask around, see if anyone else's invention was stolen."

"Speaking of stolen inventions, we still have to find Roger," Joe put in. "That's our top priority. We should get up early, get over to the gym, and start asking around."

"We have tons to do," Frank said tiredly.

"Roger's gone. Makowski was attacked. Megan was tied up, and her room was ransacked. Why?"

Phil was looking totally baffled. "Do you guys think these things are connected?"

"We don't know," Joe told him. "We could be looking at one case, or two, or three."

Phil grabbed his head. "Too much! You're giving me a headache, Hardy. Let's drop it all until tomorrow." With that, he climbed into bed and pulled a pillow over his head.

Friday morning, after an early breakfast, Phil and the Hardys arrived at Cahill College ten minutes before the gymnasium was due to open. Teenagers loaded down with boxes and weird-looking objects stood on the snow-covered sidewalk. Most of the faces were new. Joe guessed they were people who hadn't been able to make it the night before because of the bad weather.

"Guys, I'm worried. If we don't find Roger by ten o'clock, we're out of the competition," Phil said, hunching down into his parka. "That's only two hours from now."

"That's when the judges start their rounds to choose the semifinalists?" Joe inquired.

Phil nodded. "Yeah. Then the exhibits open to the public this afternoon. The winner is chosen tomorrow."

"Well, let's get to work," Frank said as the doors to the gym opened. "Phil, take the doors.

Question everyone who walks through. Joe, you and I can split up and scout the aisles again."

The boys went into the gym. Makowski was there, fiddling with the doorstop. When he saw the Hardys, he reached out and touched Joe's sleeve. "I just wanted to thank you for saving me last night," he said, smiling.

"No problem, sir," Joe said, extending his hand to shake. He loosened his grip as Makowski winced in pain. Looking down, Joe saw that the man's hand was bandaged. "Are you all right?"

"Yes." Makowski stuck his injured hand in his pocket. "I cracked my hand on the rail falling over. Overall, though, I feel pretty good. Now, if you'll excuse me, I've got to get back to piles of paperwork." He started to hurry off.

"Sir?" Frank called after him. When Makowski stopped, Frank quickly explained about their robot.

Makowski clicked his tongue sympathetically. "I saw the report this morning. You guys are in a bind. Ari Zorba insists that you can't compete without the invention present, even with specs and support material."

"But it's not our fault our robot was stolen," Frank protested.

"I know." Makowski looked embarrassed. "Look, I can give you an extra half hour off the top to look for it. But if you need more time than that, we'll have to take it up with Ari."

"Half an hour?" Joe blurted out. "That's it?"

"I'm sorry," Makowski said. "I can't change Ari's rules. I will talk to him, though. I'll also hold a meeting to deal with the problem of theft. We'll get to the bottom of this. Three o'clock, okay?" Before they could answer, Makowski strode away.

Phil rolled his eyes. "That was a big help," he said sarcastically.

"He's trying," Frank said. "He's probably got a lot on his mind, what with someone trying to kill him, you know?"

Phil looked embarrassed. "You're right."

"We didn't even ask him about that," Joe pointed out. "I'll pin him down as soon as I can."

Phil stationed himself at the door. Frank took the aisles to the right of the door, while Joe took those to the left.

Joe wandered up and down the aisles peering into booths and talking to inventors. But no one seemed to know anything about Roger. Finally Joe was in the last aisle. It was deserted. As far as he could tell, none of the booths was in use.

Joe turned around and retraced his steps. As he walked back up the aisle, he heard a woman's voice coming from one of the booths up ahead saying softly and urgently, "Did you do it?"

A young man's muffled voice answered, "I'm working on it. But I hit a snag last night."

Joe slowed down and silently crept closer.

60

Could they be talking about the robot? Or maybe even about the attacks on Makowski or Megan?

"Well, in a couple of days it'll be over—"

As Joe was about to sneak into the booth next to the voices, they stopped. A young woman stepped into the aisle. It was Tanya Zane, the judge. Behind her was Yueh, her school buddy.

Joe caught the quick look of surprise that flickered over their faces. Tanya tossed her hair to the side and quickly plastered a smile to her face. "This isn't your aisle, is it?"

Joe smiled back. "No, I was just looking for a friend."

Tanya's eyes narrowed. "Who were you looking for? There aren't any inventors in this row. The school set up too many booths."

Joe felt like asking them what *they* were doing in that aisle, but he knew that was a bad idea. Whatever Tanya and Yueh were up to, there were other ways to find out, and he didn't want to mess up Frank and Phil's chances of winning by making one of the judges mad.

So he said, "I was looking for Kara Melia."

Tanya studied him coolly. After a moment she said, "Her booth's by the center aisle. Well, excuse me. I should start my rounds."

Thinking fast, Joe reached out and touched her elbow. "Hey, can I ask you a question?"

"Tanya, I've got to get going," Yueh mumbled as he disappeared.

"Make it quick," Tanya told Joe. She began to tap her foot impatiently. "I don't have much time before the judging."

"My brother and his friend are in this competition, and last night their invention was stolen. What can we do?" Joe watched her closely to see if she reacted at all to his words.

She didn't seem to. "You're not the only ones with problems," she said. "Yueh, the guy I was just talking to, had his invention stolen, too. Lucky for him he had a prototype to replace it. Why don't you speak to Zorba? He might extend the deadline to give you more time to find it."

"Zorba?" Joe was surprised. "I'd think that Makowski would be a better bet."

"Hah! Good luck," Tanya sneered.

Before Joe could ask her what she meant, she strode off. Joe went to find Phil and Frank.

Phil caught up with him a couple of aisles down. "Any luck?" Joe asked.

"None on the robot. But I did hear something interesting. This guy Yueh Chu's invention was stolen yesterday, too."

"Yeah, I heard," Joe commented.

"But did you know that his invention is an accessory for rock climbers?" Phil's thin face was excited. "Get this—it's a lightweight launcher that shoots spikes into rock!"

Joe stared. "It shoots spikes into rock? It's got to be the thing Frank found last night. Maybe the inventor adapted it to shoot arrows."

Phil nodded. Then he looked down at his watch and gasped. "It's ten-fifteen already—and no Roger. It looks as if we're going to have to quit, Joe," he said quietly.

Phil looked utterly depressed. Joe clapped him on the shoulder. "Let's find Frank."

They ran into him at the beginning of their aisle. "I just asked Zorba for more time," Frank said heavily. "No go. As of ten-thirty, we're history, guys."

Trying to make his brother feel better, Joe told him about Phil's find with the rock-climbing invention and his own encounter with Tanya Zane.

"So Yueh's rock-climbing accessory was stolen, too," Frank said thoughtfully.

"Maybe. Or maybe he's just telling people it was stolen, but really he used it to try to shoot Mak—" Joe began.

Then, in the middle of his sentence, he stopped in his tracks. "Hey, guys. Do I see what I think I see?" he asked excitedly.

There on the table was their robot and a pile of Phil's tools!

The guys sprinted down the last few feet of their aisle. It really was Roger the Lobber. Rubbing the robot on its metallic head, Frank asked, "Where did you come from? And who stole you?"

"I don't know, and I don't care! I just want to

see if this baby works," Phil said, already tinkering with the robot.

A few minutes later, he raised his head. "It looks as if everything's fine. Ready, Roger?"

He flipped the remote on and pushed the Fetch button, while Frank tossed the ball down the aisle. Everyone heaved a sigh of relief as the robot began to whir. It started rolling toward the ball. Phil wiped his brow. "Whew!"

Suddenly, the robot veered away from the ball. Frank grabbed the remote from Phil and flicked the switch off. When nothing happened, he flipped it back and forth. Frantically, he pushed the Fetch button. Still, Roger didn't respond.

"The switch is stuck!" Frank yelled as Roger continued rolling. It rammed into a table. The table, with someone's invention on top of it, crashed to the floor.

The robot whirled around and made strange squeaky noises. Then it started rolling again, picking up speed. This time it was headed for the Sobba booth in the center aisle—zooming straight toward the multimillion-dollar computer!

7 Ambushed!

"Look out!" someone in Sobba's booth yelled.

"Stop that thing!" someone else screamed.

Frank sprinted after Roger. Hurtling over the fallen table, he closed in and tackled the robot just inches from the computer. He knocked the robot onto its side so that its wheels spun harmlessly in the air.

Phil dashed over to the furiously grinding and bleeping robot and hit the manual off switch on its side.

"That was close," Joe said.

Frank wiped his sweaty forehead. "Now we know what happened when our robot was stolen. It was sabotaged," he growled.

A man came out of the Sobba booth. "Are you

boys all right? We saw what happened. You saved our computer!" he exclaimed.

"Yeah, we're fine," Frank said. He patted the robot. "But I think we have some apologizing and some emergency robot repairs to do."

Leaving Phil to fix Roger, the Hardys went to see if their neighbor's invention was okay.

As Frank propped up the fallen table, an angry voice said, "So you're the jerks who knocked my invention over! I'm going to bust your . . ."

The Hardys swung around to see a fuming young man planted in the aisle. A name tag stuck to his sweater read Hi, I'm Cory.

"We didn't do it on purpose," Joe said. "Someone tampered with our robot. It just went crazy!"

Cory sneered. "That's what they all say."

"It's the truth," Joe insisted.

"Look, man, we're really sorry," Frank said quickly. "If there's anything we can do—pay for parts or help with the repairs—we'd be glad."

The young inventor bent over his device, which looked like a camp stove with a fishbowl on top. After a moment he peered up at the Hardys. "You're in luck. I don't think it broke."

"Great. What is it, anyway?" Frank asked.

Cory pushed his glasses up on his nose. "It's a camp stove that doubles as a clothing warmer for mountain climbers," he said proudly.

"Oh . . . very, uh, different," Frank said. He couldn't think of anything else to say.

Joe hid a snicker by coughing loudly. "Come on, bro, we'd better get back," he said.

"Right." Frank thumped Cory on the shoulder. "Good luck with the contest."

The brothers headed off. Joe was laughing quietly. "'Very, uh, different,'" he mimicked.

At their booth, Phil was making final adjustments. "Roger's going to be all right," he reported. "But guess what? I'm still missing my most useful tool, the mini-screwdriver."

Frank looked thoughtful. "That may be our only clue to Roger's thief. Here, I'll help you get the little guy going."

"I'm going to see if I can talk to Makowski," Joe said. "Maybe our luck is finally changing."

When he got to the TIC office, the receptionist told him Makowski was in a meeting. Joe sank down on a chair in the converted classroom.

As he waited, he thought about the robot thief. Why had Roger been returned? Whoever stole it obviously didn't want the robot or even want to keep Phil and Frank from competing. It seemed to be a simple prank.

At that moment, the door to the cochairs' office flew open and Tanya Zane stormed out. Joe stood up, but she brushed by him without a word and disappeared down the hall. Nicholas Makowski followed at a leisurely pace.

"Hi, Joe. What can I do for you?" he asked.

"Give me a couple minutes," Joe replied.

Makowski held out a hand to usher Joe into his office. "So what's on your mind?" he asked.

"Sir, what happened to you last night was no accident," Joe said flatly. "Someone shot an arrow at you from the observation deck. We found the weapon." He paused as Makowski raised his eyebrow. "Mr. Makowski, I hate to ask, but can you think of anyone who might want to kill you?"

Makowski's face was troubled. "So it's come to this," he said softly. "I hoped I could handle it without a fuss, but . . ." He trailed off.

Joe took a step forward. "Handle what? Tanya Zane?" he asked. "She didn't look too happy just now, and I've gotten the feeling she doesn't like you very much. Do you think she's the one who tried to kill you?"

"Tanya?" Makowski said, sounding genuinely surprised. "I don't think so. Oh, she's not too fond of me—she worked as an intern for my company last summer, and I had to let her go, for reasons that I'd rather not go into. But I doubt she'd try to kill me. No, I was thinking of . . ."

"Of who?" Joe demanded.

Makowski sighed. "Megan Sweetwater."

Joe frowned. "What makes you say that?"

"She's a very driven girl," Makowski said. He looked down, fiddling with a pen on his desk. "Maybe even a bit unbalanced. She's convinced someone's out to steal that leash of hers, and she thinks I'm not taking it seriously enough."

"That hardly seems like a reason to try to kill you," Joe argued. "Anyway, she says she wasn't nearby when you were shot at."

"But I saw her," Makowski said.

"What?" Joe cried incredulously.

"I saw her," Makowski repeated. "Or a girl who looked just like her. She was climbing up to the observation deck right before I went over."

Joe's heart sank. Had Megan been lying to them? Or could Makowski be mistaken?

"Look." Makowski's voice broke into his thoughts. "Let's keep this conversation between us for now. It was dark, after all, and I can't be sure of what I saw. That's why I didn't say anything about it last night. Anyway, I'd like the chance to try to work things out unofficially before we call in the police. I can't believe Megan could really want to kill me. I'm sure we can clear things up."

"Sounds good," Joe said, smiling. "Thanks. We'll see what we can find out on our end, too."

"Good, good," Makowski said. "Now, was there anything else?"

"Oh, I almost forgot," Joe said. Quickly he told Makowski about the sabotaged robot.

"So the Sobba computer was undamaged? What a relief! Once again, the Hardy brothers save the day," Makowski said, smiling. "Well, we'll get to the bottom of this mess at the meeting this afternoon, I promise. All six judges will be there, as well as Ari and myself." He stood up.

"Great!" Joe headed for the door.

"Oh, Joe, as for the arrow launcher, please drop it in my office as soon as possible," Makowski added. "If we do have to take this case to the police, they'll want to see it."

"Right. See you later," Joe said as he left.

When he got back to the booth, he found Frank and Phil giving each other high fives. "We fixed it!" Phil crowed.

"Hey, that's great!" Joe said.

"It turned out to be a simple, extremely clever rewiring of one of Roger's circuits," Frank told Joe. "And, of course, the remote was broken. So what did Makowski say?"

Joe's smile faded. Quickly he told the other two what Makowski had said about Megan.

Phil was indignant. "I don't believe it," he said. "He couldn't tell who it was going up the ladder. It was dark! It could have been anyone."

Joe sighed. Then he brightened a little. "Hey, maybe someone is out to frame Megan," he suggested.

"Why?" Frank objected. "What's the point?"

Joe shrugged. "You got me."

"What did Makowski say about the arrow launcher?" Frank asked after a short silence.

"He wants us to give it to him for evidence," Joe said. "I—" Then he stopped, frowning. Something was bothering him, but he couldn't put his finger on what it was.

At that moment, a voice on the loudspeaker

blared, "Judging will continue after a one-hour lunch break. All judges are requested to leave the floor now."

"Lunch break? Sounds good—I'm starved," Joe said, rubbing his belly. "Let's go!"

Taking no chances, Frank and Phil quickly dismantled Roger and packed him in his case. Then they headed for the cafeteria, which was in a nearby annex.

"You guys order for me," Frank said as they left the gym. "I'm going to check the college library for info on Preton, Inc."

In the cafeteria, Phil and Joe piled food on their plates and on an extra one for Frank, and went to sit down by the window.

"Hey, it's Megan and her cute little puppy dog."

Joe muttered, "Yeah, right. Man's best friend."

Megan smiled when she saw the two and commanded Bunny to heel. "Hi, guys. How's the food? Mine was awful."

"How are you doing?" Joe asked, noting that she looked pretty tired.

Megan sighed. "I've been better. At least I haven't been threatened by anybody today."

"Yeah, well, get this," Phil said before Joe was able to stop him. "We found your dog's hairs in the contraption that was used to attack Mr. Makowski. And Makowski thinks you tried to kill him."

"What?" Megan turned pale.

Joe sighed. Then he quickly brought her up to date on the case, trying to downplay Makowski's accusation as much as possible. "He isn't at all sure of what he saw," he said gently. "And even if he did see someone who looks like you, it could be that someone is trying to frame you.

"Anyway, Frank is checking out the Preton company now," he added. "We'll know more in a few minutes. Don't worry, we'll work it all out."

"I know," she said with a weak smile. She sank into a seat across from Phil.

"Hey, there's Frank now." Phil stood up and waved him over to the table.

When Frank saw his plate of food, his eyes lit up. Popping a forkful in his mouth, he mumbled, "First things first."

"What about Preton? Did you find anything?" his brother pressed.

"Let me swallow this bite," Frank protested.

"Okay, okay." Joe grinned. "Never come between a man and his meal."

A few minutes later, Frank wiped his mouth with a napkin and said, "You want to know what I learned about Preton?"

Everyone at the table nodded.

"Absolutely nothing. It doesn't exist."

Joe stared. "What do you mean?"

"I mean, it's a fictitious company. At least it's not registered in any directory. I even made a call to Con Riley in Bayport. He called a few sources and got back to me," Frank said.

"So that's a dead end," Megan said softly.

Looking at her stricken face, Joe smiled. "Hey, it's not a dead end. We know more than we did. We know that Preton doesn't exist."

"Yeah—which makes it seem even more as if I made the whole story up," Megan said bitterly.

"No," Phil protested. "You sure didn't make up being stuffed into that rocket."

"That's true," Megan repeated listlessly. "Look, I'll see you guys later." She flipped her hand up in a halfhearted wave and left. Bunny trotted behind her.

Frank cleared his throat. "I just want to tell you guys—I think someone *is* trying to frame Megan. There are just too many coincidences that make her look bad and, as you said, Phil, there's no question someone stuffed her in that rocket. She couldn't do it herself."

"All right!" Joe grinned at his brother. "About time you figured that out."

"The question is," Frank went on, "who's doing this to her, and why?"

There was a glum silence. Then Phil said, "We'd better get back. One of the judges said we were her first stop."

Back in the gym, Joe asked, "Frank, where did you put the launcher? What if I try to find Yueh and ask him about it, then drop the thing

73

off to Makowski while you two deal with the judges?"

"Good idea. The launcher's at the hotel. And don't forget the meeting at three."

Twenty minutes later, Joe, with the launcher and arrow in a paper bag, went to Yueh's booth. But the display table was bare, and there was no one around. After searching the gym without success, Joe decided to try the cafeteria. As he walked out, he saw Makowski at the Sobba booth.

Joe held up the bag. "I'll leave this with your receptionist," he called. Makowski nodded.

"Going somewhere?" a voice murmured.

Joe whirled. Byron stood behind him with a faint, cocky smile on his face. "What's in the bag?" Byron asked, making a grab for Joe's package.

"Nothing for you," Joe said curtly, and moved away. Byron sure knew how to be annoying!

As he walked down the hall toward the cafeteria annex, Joe wondered why it seemed so deserted. He figured it out when he got to the cafeteria and found the doors locked.

"Rats. Must be two o'clock already," he muttered, and started back.

All of a sudden, he got a creepy feeling. Was someone following him? Joe turned his head quickly. No one was behind him. The corridor on his right was empty.

I'm jumpy, he thought. Pushing the eerie feeling out of his mind, he threw his shoulders back and continued walking down the hall.

Suddenly Joe heard a stealthy footstep behind him. A split second later something thudded sharply against his skull. White stars exploded in front of his eyes.

Then he slumped to the ground, unconscious.

8 Who's Messing with Whom?

Joe winced and opened his eyes to total black-ness. His head was throbbing.

"Hooooo," he groaned, and realized his mouth was gagged with tape. He was leaning back against a wall, propped on what felt like a turned-over bucket. He tried to move his arms, but they were tied behind his back. His ankles burned where the rope cut into them.

Joe's cramped body started to sag to the side. He gently bumped against another wall as he struggled to stay seated on his perch.

I must be in a closet, he thought. He tested his theory by leaning in the other direction. When he hit another side wall in the narrow space, his immediate thought was to bang on the door so someone would find him.

As he moved forward and tried to stand up, something sharp pricked into his chest. He jerked back, falling hard on the bucket and hitting his head on the back wall. He could feel blood trickling down his skin.

What is that? he thought. He moved forward again, this time much more slowly. The pointed object pierced him again. Whatever it was, it was really sharp. He sank back down to his original position.

Someone sure doesn't want me to bang on that door, he thought. The blood trickled steadily down, sticking his shirt to his skin.

In the gym, Phil and Frank were busy with a steady stream of judges, reporters, and the few members of the public who had wandered in.

Now Tanya Zane was striding up with a small notebook. Without looking at Frank or Phil, she examined Roger and scratched down notes.

"I knew your invention would turn up," she said as she wrote. "What's this Fetch button?" She frowned and held up the remote device to the light. "How does it work?"

Phil explained the remote control they had developed for their robot. Frank watched Tanya as his partner talked. She didn't seem to be paying attention. His thoughts went back to her comments. Why had she asked about the remote in particular? Frank wondered if she knew the

77

remote had been sabotaged. And how had she known the robot would show up?

"That was terrible last night, wasn't it?" Frank asked.

"What was terrible?" Tanya gave him a puzzled look. "Oh, you mean Makowski's accident?"

"That's right, only it wasn't an accident."

"What do you mean?" Tanya asked suspiciously.

"Well, we found something that looks like Yueh's rock-climbing invention on the ship. Apparently it was used to shoot an arrow at Mr. Makowski," Frank said, watching Tanya closely for her reaction. "It makes me wonder . . ."

"What are you implying?" Tanya interrupted, her eyes narrowing to slits. "Are you saying that Yueh shot Makowski?"

"Not at all," Frank said. Obviously he'd hit a sore spot. "We just want to help. I mean, it'd be terrible if Yueh were accused of shooting that arrow. He could clear his name if we knew where he had been last night."

The judge slammed her notebook shut. "What business is this of yours, anyway? For your information, Yueh wasn't on that ship. He and I were both—busy—somewhere else." She looked uncomfortable for a moment. Then she went on. "Anyway, he couldn't have done it. His invention had been stolen earlier that afternoon. Ask Ari Zorba. He's got the report." She whipped around and marched down the aisle.

Phil whistled. "Do you think this means she likes us?"

Frank laughed, then turned serious. "She's very defensive. I wonder if she and Yueh are after Makowski together. They could have planted those hairs—Megan's dog's hairs—in the launcher and pretended it was stolen to get themselves off the suspect list."

"But why?" Phil asked. "We know she doesn't like Makowski for some personal reasons. But why would Yueh be involved? Could she have promised to get the judges to vote for him?"

"Could be. I didn't see either of them on the ship last night. Did you?"

Phil shook his head silently.

"Did they sneak on and stay hidden until the incident?" Frank continued, thinking aloud. "If they weren't on board, where were they? Maybe Joe learned something from Yueh—" Frank stopped suddenly. "Phil, what time is it?"

"Two-thirty. Hey, Joe's not back," Phil replied, realizing what Frank was getting at.

"Yup. He should have talked to Yueh and been back here a while ago. I'm going to look for him. If, for some reason, I'm not back by three, go to the meeting and tell our story."

"Yes, boss," Phil agreed with a mock bow.

Frank began looking up and down the aisles, hoping his brother was checking out the other inventions.

"Maybe he's with Byron," Kara Melia suggested when Frank went to her booth. "I saw them talking together about a half hour ago."

"Thanks." Frank headed for Byron's booth. When he got there, though, no one was around. On the table, Byron's invention was humming.

Why would he leave his machine on? Frank wondered. Maybe something made him leave quickly. But what?

Just then the machine, which was shaped like an old-fashioned typewriter, started to spit out a sheet of heavy, wet paper.

Neither Byron nor Joe was anywhere to be seen. Frank wanted to shut it off, but didn't dare touch it. He didn't want to be accused of sabotage again.

He turned back toward the center aisle—and stopped in his tracks.

A figure was huddled behind the table in a booth across the aisle. It was Byron. And he was tinkering with someone's invention. Frank looked up and down the aisle. No one could see Byron. He was out of the line of sight.

A girl walked by, and Frank touched her on the arm. "Get security!" he whispered. When she saw Frank's serious expression, she took off running.

Frank silently crept over to the booth where Byron was crouched down. He watched Byron. The guy was sabotaging someone's invention!

Stepping inside the booth, Frank demanded, "Just what are you doing?"

Byron jerked up his head. He ran his eyes up and down Frank's body. Slowly, he got to his feet and walked over to Frank. "What's it to you?" he said with a sneer. He raised his arm quickly and reached for the top of Frank's head.

Frank threw his forearm into Byron's hand, blocking his movement.

"Hey, don't get so testy!" Byron cracked a grin, and slowly withdrew his arm. "I was only going to ruffle your hair."

"Look, Byron, if you're messing around with someone's invention . . ."

"How do you know I'm doing anything wrong?" Byron demanded. He crossed his arms across his chest. "Well, Mr. Snoop? Mr. Comet Expert? Huh? Tell me," he taunted.

Frank's temper flared. His hands clenched into fists by his side. "It's not cool to mess with other people's stuff," he said through gritted teeth.

"What's going on?" said a shrill voice.

Byron winked to someone behind Frank. Frank stepped backward, never letting his eyes leave Byron. He pivoted sideways so that he could see Byron and the other person at the same time.

It was a short young woman with curly blond hair. "I said, what is going on here? Who is this guy, Byron?" she demanded loudly.

Byron laughed. "Tess, meet Frank Hardy."

Tess sniffed. "What's he doing here? I don't know you, Frank. What are you doing in my booth? What's going on?"

"Your booth?" Frank said, relaxing his muscles. "This is your booth?"

"Are you deaf?" Tess cried.

Frank gritted his teeth again. "Look, I just saw Byron kneeling over your invention, and I wanted to make sure he wasn't—"

"Wasn't what? Sabotaging it? Everyone is so paranoid around here! Did you ever think that I might have asked Byron to help me fix my driving simulator?" Tess demanded, wiping a speck of dust off the invention. "He happens to be brilliant with electronics."

"I'm sorry," Frank said. "Believe it or not, I was trying to do you a favor."

Heavy steps echoed down the aisle. "What's going on here?" a gruff voice asked.

Frank gave an inward groan. It was the same guard who'd been so difficult the night before. "Just a misunderstanding, sir. I thought someone was sabotaging this girl's invention."

"He's going around accusing people without any proof!" Tess huffed.

The guard frowned. "You," he said, pointing at Frank, "are a troublemaker. Do I have to haul you in to the office *again?*"

Byron started snickering.

Tess looked a little calmer. "Hey, it's okay," she mumbled. "No harm done."

"Sure, now? If I have to come back to break up a fight, you are all in trouble. Especially you," the guard warned, pointing to Frank.

"Don't even think of it," Byron said lightly. "We're back to being buddies, aren't we, Frank?"

"Sure," Frank said, stone-faced. The guard turned on his heels and left.

Frank was walking away when Byron tapped his shoulder.

"Look, man," Byron said. "No hard feelings. You're taking this whole thing way too seriously. Can't people have fun anymore?" He shrugged.

"Sure." Frank forced a smile. He didn't feel like keeping up the fight. He was also getting more worried about Joe. Where was he? "You haven't seen Joe, have you?" he asked.

"Not lately," Byron told him. "Last I saw him he was going that-a-way." He pointed toward the cafeteria.

Frank left for the cafeteria. Finding it closed, he decided to try the TIC office.

"Can I help you?" the receptionist asked when Frank stepped up to the desk.

"I was just wondering—" Frank began.

Just then a janitor dashed into the room, waving his arms. "There's something"—he gulped for breath—"something in my closet!"

"What do you mean?" Frank was suddenly alert.

"I heard something moving. It sounded big. Really big! And I tried the door, but it was locked. It was open when I left it an hour ago," the man said wildly. "I never lock that door!"

"I'll send security with the keys. Which closet?" the receptionist asked.

"Down that hall." The janitor pointed. "Near the cafeteria. Instead of going straight, take the first right. It's about halfway down."

Frank ran out of the office in the direction of the closet. Behind him the receptionist yelled, "Come back! Wait for security!"

But Frank was already racing down the stairs. When he got to the closet door, he stuck his ear to it. No noises came from inside. He grasped the doorknob and turned it slowly. Locked.

Then he heard it. Thump. Thump. Thump. The muffled sound came from the floor, as if someone was stomping his feet on the ground.

"Hey," he called into the wooden door. "Can you hear me? Joe?"

The thumping grew more frantic. Frank wrenched the doorknob to the right, but it wouldn't turn.

At that moment a security guard bustled up with a clanking ring of keys. "Step aside, son," she said importantly.

Frank moved aside, and the guard began fitting keys into the lock. After several wrong tries, she found the right one. She yanked the door open. Frank sucked in his breath as his brother tumbled out of the closet. His long-sleeved T-shirt had a bloody stain on the front.

"Oh my," the guard said faintly.

"Joe!" Frank stooped down and began to untie his brother's bonds.

When the tape was removed from his mouth, Joe groaned. He squeezed out a weak smile. "Glad to see you," he whispered.

"What happened to you?" Frank demanded. "Man, are you okay?" He placed his jacket under Joe's head. Gently pulling up his brother's stained shirt, Frank was relieved to see that the wound was clean and shallow.

"I'll call a doctor," the guard said, looking rather green. She hurried down the hall.

"The door," Joe mumbled. He made a slight movement in the direction of the closet door.

Frank looked over at the door, which was gaping open. He had been so concerned with his brother, he hadn't seen the arrow crudely stuck to the wood with wads of duct tape. It was the same kind as the red-tipped, clear-stemmed arrow that had been shot at Makowski!

Frank whistled. A piece of paper hung from the arrow. He pulled the bloody-tipped weapon off the door and, with it, the heavy, grayish paper.

"This is Byron's paper!" he exclaimed. Crouching down to let his brother see, Frank examined the textured page. Together, the Hardys read the typed words: MIND YOUR OWN BUSINESS OR PREPARE TO PAY!

9 A Safe Explosion?

"Someone's getting nervous," Frank muttered, pocketing the arrow and note. "We must be heading in the right direction. I can't wait to bust them after this stunt!"

He helped his brother to a sitting position. "What happened to you?"

"Someone slugged me on the back of the head. What a monster headache!" Joe said, wincing. He grasped Frank's arm. "The launcher—I had it with me. Is it in there?"

Frank quickly checked the floor of the broom closet. The bag with the launcher was nowhere to be found.

Before they could discuss it, the guard came back with a tall, dark-skinned man with a black leather bag. "Here's the doctor. I'm going to get you some water. Be right back," Frank said, sprinting off to the cafeteria for a cup.

"Let me take a look at that wound," said the doctor.

Joe pulled up his shirt. "I don't think it's serious. Just a scratch that bled a lot," he said.

"You're right," the doctor said after examining the wound. "I'll just wipe the area with iodine to ward off infection. Do you have pain anywhere else?" he asked.

"I'm okay," Joe lied. Actually, his head was pounding, and he knew there was a lump behind his left ear, but he didn't want to get into it with the doctor. Doctors always told you to get plenty of rest—and he didn't have time to rest right now!

"Here you go, Joe." Frank handed him a paper cup of water, which he gulped down gratefully.

"Can you stand?" the doctor asked.

With Frank's help, Joe staggered to his feet.

"I'm just a little shaken up," he murmured as he waited for the walls to stop spinning. "It's pretty cool to see double like this!"

The security guard and the doctor stepped off into the corner, where all the Hardys could hear was the buzz of the guard's radio.

"Now. Who knew you had the launcher with you?" Frank asked quietly.

"No one!" Joe protested. "I couldn't find Yueh to talk to him, so obviously he didn't know. I saw Makowski on my way here, but he wouldn't steal

87

the launcher—I was bringing it to him anyway. And—wait!" He snapped his fingers. "Byron!"

Frank leaned forward. "Byron?"

"Yeah, he seemed really interested in what I had in the bag," Joe said. "I didn't tell him, but maybe he guessed."

"Byron keeps popping up today." Frowning, Frank told Joe about his own encounter with Byron.

"So he's an electronics whiz, eh?" Joe said thoughtfully. "Think he sabotaged Roger?"

"Maybe. And it looks as if we'll have to add him to the list of people who might have shot at Makowski," Frank added. "Though I don't know what his motive could be."

Just then the guard came up to the brothers. "Son, we'll need you to make a statement to the police," she told Joe. "You feel up to it?"

He groaned. "I guess so."

"While you're doing that, I'll catch the rest of the student sabotage meeting." Frank nudged his brother's arm, and, with the guard following, they walked to the TIC office.

Joe sank down on a chair and waited for the police, while the receptionist showed Frank into the meeting room.

Eleven heads turned toward Frank as he entered. He noted that Yueh was at the table, along with Megan and Phil, Zorba, Makowski, and the six judges. Tanya glared at him.

"Glad you could make it," Zorba said with

heavy sarcasm. "Hope we're not taking up too much of your valuable time."

"Sorry. My brother ran into some trouble—"

Phil's eyes widened.

Zorba cut Frank off. "Hmph. Let's continue. Megan, you were saying . . . ?"

Megan looked close to tears. She played with one of her silver hoop earrings as she spoke. "I was just told that someone planted dog hairs in Yueh's invention, which was used to shoot an arrow at Mr. Makowski last night. Someone's trying to frame me!" She glared at Yueh.

A few of the judges gasped. Makowski was scrawling notes on a yellow pad.

Yueh jumped to his feet. "What was that? My invention was used to do what?"

"Drop your innocent act, Yueh. 'It was used to do what?'" Megan imitated sarcastically.

Frank watched Yueh. The inventor's look of confusion turned to rage. Pounding his fist on the table, he yelled, "You're saying that I rigged my rock-climbing invention to shoot Mr. Makowski? Why would I do that?"

"You tell me," Megan retorted.

His face was red. "You, you little—"

"People, people!" Makowski called sharply. "Please!" He looked at Megan. "Don't you think you're getting carried away?" he asked. "Yueh has no motive to kill me."

Tears welled up in her eyes and spilled down her cheeks. "Neither do I! But you don't believe me! No one believes me!" Sobbing, she shoved her chair back and ran from the room.

There was an uncomfortable silence. One of the judges tapped her fingers against the table.

Frank turned to Yueh. "Can you tell us where you were last night? Were you on the cruise?"

Yueh shot a furtive glance at Tanya, then looked down. "No, I didn't go on the cruise," he mumbled. "I had something else to do."

"What?" Frank persisted.

"Really!" Zorba interrupted angrily. "Who gave you the right to ask questions, Mr. Hardy?"

"I'm only trying to—" Frank started.

"Spare me," Zorba growled. "I've had enough of your grandstanding."

"Ari!" Makowski protested.

Zorba glared at him. "Obviously you think I'm being too harsh."

Makowski sighed. "With respect, I realize you ran the entire show last year and that you have more experience than I do, but—"

Zorba stood up. "Exactly," he said forcefully. With that, he turned sharply and strode out of the room.

After the door stopped shaking in the frame, Makowski looked around. "Maybe we'd better call it a day," he murmured.

Everyone got up and filed out. Joe stood up when he saw his friends enter the lobby.

Phil stared in horror at the bloodstain on Joe's shirt. "Are you all right?" he cried.

"I'm tired of explaining what happened, but physically, I'm fine." Joe frowned. "What's with Megan?" he asked. "She ran out of here in tears. She didn't even stop when I called her."

Frank told Joe about the scene at the meeting. "Things are getting hairy," he went on. "And I'm wondering if we shouldn't add a new name to our list of suspects in the Makowski shooting."

"Zorba?" Joe said.

Frank nodded. "He could have easily hidden the remote control for the launcher in his pocket. And he sure doesn't like Makowski much."

"Let's look into it," Joe said. "How can we find out whether he rigged the launcher or not?"

"Slow down! Let's go back to the hotel first," Frank said. "We can get cleaned up and figure out our next move."

"Hey, you're forgetting something, aren't you?" Phil said, holding up Roger's carrying case. "Partner, don't you want to hear how Roger killed all the competition?"

Frank's face broke into a smile. He checked his watch. "Four-twenty. They'll be announcing the semifinalists in about ten minutes."

The guys hurried back to the gym. Inventors were everywhere, milling excitedly. The tension mounted as the loudspeaker started crackling. As a judge read down the list of ten semifinalists, the boys could hear cheers or groans coming from different sections of the gym.

Then Frank's and Phil's names were read.

91

"Whoo-ie!" Phil yelped. Patting Roger's case, he did a little victory dance. "What'd I tell you? Pretty hot invention! Pretty hot inventors!" he exclaimed, patting Frank on the back.

Byron, Yueh, and Megan also made it to the finals. "Wow," Phil commented. "Out of ten semifinalists, we know half of them."

Megan came up to them. "Congrats!" she said, hugging Frank and Phil. Bunny thumped his tail.

"You, too," Frank said. Megan's eyes were red, but she looked calm. Hearing her name on the list of semifinalists had probably helped.

The four friends decided to take off. It was so frigid outside they jogged back to the hotel to keep warm. Megan agreed to meet them for dinner at the hotel restaurant at six-thirty and went to put Bunny in the pet holding room.

"I call first shower," Joe shouted as the guys got off the elevator at their floor.

"I guess," Phil drawled, "that someone who got whacked over the head and pierced in the chest does deserve to shower before, say, a top robot designer."

Joe swiped at Phil, then practically dived into the bathroom with his towel. While he was showering, Frank updated Phil on Joe's attack in the hall. Joe stepped out of the bathroom as Frank was showing Phil the threatening note on Byron's stationery and the arrow he had found in the closet with Joe.

"So Byron did it?" Phil asked, wide-eyed.

"He's a suspect," Frank hedged. "But what's his motive? And why would someone as smart as Byron use paper from his own invention?"

"Too many clues point to too many people," Joe complained. "All we know is that whoever our bad guys are, they have great access to all the inventions."

Frank nodded. "If Yueh and Tanya are working together, they would have all the information at their fingertips."

"So would Zorba," Joe added.

Frank stretched wearily. "Well, we've got a lot to do tonight at the Sears Tower social. We'll pin Yueh and Tanya down about where they were last night during the cruise. And we should see if we can find out anything about Zorba."

"Also, we should keep an eye on Byron, just in case," Joe put in.

Phil flicked his hair out of his eyes. Glancing at his watch, he groaned. "We were supposed to meet Megan five minutes ago. I guess we'll have to grab showers later, Frank."

The guys hurried downstairs, worried that Megan would be waiting. But she came up to them just as got to the lobby. "Sorry I'm late," she said breathlessly. "I had to feed Bunny."

"You look great!" Phil said admiringly. Megan was dressed for the evening in a black jumpsuit and gold earrings.

She blushed. "Thanks. I figured it's time I pulled myself together and started having fun."

The four teenagers found a window table and ordered two deep-dish stuffed pizzas.

"Things still quiet, Megan?" Joe asked.

"So far, no more phone calls or attacks," she answered. "I'm keeping my fingers crossed."

Phil, who had been watching the doors to the kitchen, started rubbing his hands together. "Here comes our pizza. Wow, that was fast!"

The smell of the steaming pies made their mouths water. The waiter cut the pizza, revealing insides laden with pepperoni and gooey cheese.

"So this is the famous Chicago pizza? I'll test it first, just to make sure it's not poisonous," Phil said, sticking his plate out.

"Hey, ladies first," Megan said, grabbing the spatula.

All of a sudden, a rumbling blast split the air. Next to Megan, the window seemed to bend outward. Then it shattered with a tinkling sound.

There was dead silence for a moment. Then someone started to scream. Frank looked through the window into the lobby. Black smoke was pouring into the room.

"Fire!" someone yelled. "Fire!"

10 Sears Tower Fiasco

A fire alarm started shrieking, and the crowd erupted in panic. Chairs flew to the ground as people ran toward the lobby. A burly man pushed a waitress over, spilling her tray of hot pizza.

When Frank saw that, he jumped on top of his seat. "Attention!" he yelled in a deep, commanding tone. "Walk, don't run!"

It was hard to be heard over the screaming alarm, but Frank kept at it. "Walk slowly to the front door. Don't panic! Everyone will get out safely if you don't panic. Walk!" he ordered.

The people looked at him with frightened faces, but they slowed down. Quickly, they moved into the lobby, then out into the street.

When the crowd was gone from the restaurant, Megan, Phil, and the Hardys ran into the lobby.

Smoke was seeping under a fire door at the back of the room. "Listen!" Megan cried.

From behind the door came frantic barking.

"It's Bunny!" Megan's voice was anguished. "The holding room is back there!"

"We'll save him," Joe shouted, running for the door. Frank was right behind him.

"I'm coming with you!" Megan yelled.

Joe, Megan, and Frank pushed through the door and ran down a hall of offices. The smoke grew thicker, but they could still breathe. A distraught bellhop ran by with a handkerchief pressed to his face. "In the manager's office!" he yelled when he saw the teenagers.

The Hardys didn't need to be told which was the manager's office. It was clearly the one whose door had been blown off its hinges. Joe peered through the doorway. "The curtains just went up," he warned. "And the rug's on fire."

Other than that, however, the fire didn't seem to have spread. Joe was relieved. He and Frank could handle this one.

"There's a kitchen with a sink farther down the hall!" Megan called. "I'm going for Bunny."

Joe skirted the flames coming from the rug. He hopped along the very edge of the room until he reached the curtains. Tearing them off the rods, he threw them to the ground and started stomping on the flames.

Frank ran into the kitchen and slammed

through several cabinets until he found a bucket. He filled it, grabbed the fire extinguisher from the wall, and ran back to the burning room.

Joe had just finished killing the flames in the curtains. He grabbed the extinguisher from Frank.

"Heads up!" Frank yelled. He drenched the rug as Joe sprayed the extinguisher back and forth. The rug sizzled and steamed.

"Move it! Out of our way!" a deep voice yelled. Several firefighters ran down the hall with a thick hose in their hands.

They stopped short at the doorway. "Hey, where's the fire?" one of them asked.

Frank stepped into the hall, wiping sweat and soot from his face. "It was in there," he said. "It wasn't that big."

The firefighters looked amused. "I guess we missed it," one of them said. They went in and started checking to make sure the fire was really out.

"Hey, Frank," Joe called. "Check this out."

Frank went over to Joe, who was crouched by the hotel safe. Its door hung by the hinges. The metal was covered with a sticky layer of soot.

Frank knelt and peered at the safe's contents.

"What are you doing?" a sharp voice demanded from above them. "Who let you in here?"

Turning, the Hardys saw a woman in a business

suit standing with her hands on her hips. "I'm Detective Novello," she told them.

At that moment, Megan came in. "Bunny's okay," she said breathlessly. "The fire didn't get—" She turned white when she saw the safe.

"My leash," she whispered. Joe reached over to steady her as she gave a devastated groan. "Quick, check, is it there?" she said urgently.

Frank shook his head.

"Oh, no," she moaned. "It's all my fault. Where will this end? Why didn't I just give the stupid thing to those callers?"

"What's going on here?" Novello asked. Frank briefly described the fire and explained why Megan was so upset.

"The safe looks as if it was blown open with a plastic explosive. As you can see, the explosion started a fire. We'll have to get the list from the hotel manager to see if Megan's leash is the only thing missing," Frank explained.

Novello stared at Frank as if he was nuts. "I suppose you're a detective as well as a firefighter?" she asked. "Do me a favor. Go give your statements to Officer Cain there. Then get out of my hair!"

Frank clenched his teeth to keep his anger from spilling over. He went to Joe and Megan, who were sitting on a charred coffee table. Joe was trying to comfort Megan.

"We're not wanted here. Let's go," Frank told

them. Then he paused, raising a finger to stop Joe's questions. Novello was talking to the manager behind them.

"Where were you when the explosion happened?" Novello was asking.

"I had gotten a phone call from someone on the eighth floor, wanting me to check out a problem in a room," the manager explained. "When I went up there, an elderly man came to the door. He didn't know anything about a phone call. But then he wanted to complain about his shower. Of course I had to stay and try to help out."

Novello scratched notes on her pad. "Do you remember anything about the caller? The one who told you to go up there?"

"Well, it was a woman," the manager recalled. "And she sounded young. But that's about all I can tell you."

Joe nudged Frank. "Could be the same one who's been calling Megan," he whispered.

Novello tossed them an irritated frown. "You kids still here? Go on, run along."

"Nice," Joe muttered as they walked out. "I can't deal with these people who won't even give us the time of day."

"Skip it," Frank advised. "It's a waste of energy to even worry about it. Anyway, we weren't going to learn any more from that site."

As they waited for the elevator, Megan cleared her throat. "Guys, I don't think I'm going to the

Sears Tower social tonight. I'm not in a partying mood," she said quietly.

"Hey," Joe said. "Remember what I told you in there? We're going to get your leash back."

Frank caught her doubting glance. "Megan, we'll have a better chance of solving this case if you help," he told her. "Besides, it'll be neat to watch the laser show. I hear they're going to use them to project music videos into the sky. You don't have to be social," he said.

Megan sighed. "All right. I'll take a shower and be up in twenty minutes." She looked down at her sooty outfit and gave a little laugh. "I'm just glad I wasn't wearing white!"

"That's the spirit! Here's your stop. See you in twenty," Joe said as the elevator doors opened on the fourth floor.

Phil was waiting for the Hardys in their room. While they were changing, Frank and Joe gave him the lowdown on what had happened.

"So who has access to explosives?" Phil asked, when they were done.

"Practically anybody," Joe replied. "That stuff isn't so hard to get. And anyone who can build one of the inventions here could definitely build a bomb." He sighed in frustration. "It doesn't eliminate any suspects."

"We should be asking who knew Megan had the leash in the safe," Frank said.

"Anyone who went to the meeting this afternoon, for starters," Joe answered.

"That excludes Byron," Frank said. "Unless he found out some other way."

Phil looked gloomy. "That guy knows everything—he has amazing sources."

"Phil's right. Byron is still on the list," Joe said.

A knock on the door interrupted the discussion. "That's Megan now," Phil said, jumping up. He threw open the door. "Let's go. We're over an hour late. If we wait any longer, there could be a major tragedy."

Megan looked alarmed. "What do you mean?"

"We could miss all the food," Phil said with a grin. "We never did get to eat that pizza!"

In the cab, Frank asked Megan what she knew of Tanya Zane.

Megan wrinkled her nose. "She and I were last year's top competitors. She wasn't very friendly." Then Megan grinned a little sheepishly. "Of course, I've heard people say the same thing about me."

"Do you know anything about her working for Makowski's company last summer?" Joe asked.

"Well, I heard Makowski fired her, but I don't know why. It was probably her attitude," Megan said. "She's very smart, but she's also got a terrible temper."

"Hmm," Joe said, with a significant glance at Frank. A temper? Maybe Makowski was wrong about Tanya—maybe she *would* try to kill him.

Just then the cab pulled up in front of the Sears Tower. "Look," Megan said, pointing up to the night sky, "they really are projecting the videos in the sky. Hey, this could be fun!"

The teenagers took a super-fast elevator to the one-hundred-third-floor skydeck, then climbed a half-flight of stairs to a room with windows on all four sides. The glass started waist-high and extended to the ceiling.

A song was blasting over the speakers as they entered. Every window was like a giant video screen. Outside, seemingly suspended in the sky, lasers created multicolored fantastic pictures that changed with the song's lyrics.

"The snack table looks like a good place to start asking questions," Frank said, eyeing the chips hungrily.

All of a sudden, the laser images melted into fuzzy pink. Then they went off completely, plunging the room into darkness. The stereo cut off. There was dead silence.

"What happened?" someone said. Another person laughed nervously.

"Let's get out of here!" a voice called.

In an instant, there was panic. Joe felt someone elbow him in the back, trying to get out of the skydeck. As the teenagers pushed each other, scrambling blindly toward the lobby, an emerald green flash lit the room.

The crowd watched, dumbstruck. Outside, the lasers flickered chaotically. Every color in the rainbow flashed in front of the Hardys' eyes. All of a sudden the speakers thundered alive. Instead of music, a hysterical laugh filled the room.

Then the crazy laser patterns stopped and formed words for all the inventors to read:

HARDYS—YOU'RE NOT WANTED HERE! GET OUT WHILE YOU STILL CAN!

11 Snagged on the Stairs

An uneasy silence hung in the air. Someone snickered and called out, "Welcome to Chicago!" A few people who stood near the snack table stared at Frank and Joe curiously.

Moving as one, Frank and Joe raced into the lobby. There were several doors. "Where are the lasers projected from?" Frank asked a man in a building uniform who was getting on the elevator.

"Up the stairs on the right," the man told him. The elevator doors slid shut.

Frank hopped up the stairs, two at a time. Joe was right behind him. They stepped into a short hallway that seemed to be a kind of upper extension of the skydeck. The narrow windowed corridor ran right along the tower's four outer walls so that it shared the same view as the skydeck below it.

Frank followed the windowed corridor to the left while Joe went to the right. Frank didn't walk far before he came upon a laser projector. It was now showing frogs jumping over trees.

There was no one attending the machine. It was automatic, Frank guessed. A preset program sent videos to the projectors and music to the speakers. But where was the programming room?

He raced around two more sides of the building, each with its own projector, and met up with Joe. "Whatever tampering was done must have been done in the programming room," Frank pointed out. "These are just projectors. I'm going to check out the other stairwell I just passed. Why don't you go back down and see if you can find Zorba or Makowski?"

"Okay. I'll check out the last projector, just in case we missed something," Joe said.

Frank returned to the stairs he had seen. The only light came from a red emergency exit sign at the bottom. On a landing halfway down was a gray steel door with a sign on it that said AU-THORIZED PERSONNEL ONLY.

"That must be the programming room," Frank said aloud. He hurried down the stairs and pulled open the door.

Inside, the room was pitch-black. To Frank's right, something rustled. He took a tentative step forward. "Hello?" he called. "Who's there?"

Suddenly someone slammed into his side, hurling him back against the doorframe. "Hey!" Frank yelled. He stuck his hands out, trying to get a grip on his attacker. His fingers latched on to an arm in what felt like a wool coat.

"Gotcha," Frank muttered. But he spoke too soon. The intruder wrenched his sleeve away with such force that his arm struck the steel door, and Frank heard a muffled yelp of pain. At the same time there was a faint pinging sound. Then the intruder launched himself at Frank's midsection. Off balance, Frank fell backward, cracking his head on a chair as he went down.

"Ooh," Frank moaned. Through pain-dimmed eyes, he saw a tall shadow race out of the room and down the stairs.

Frank lay there for a moment or two, dazed. Then he painfully climbed to his feet and felt along the wall until he found the light switch. He flicked it on.

Just then Joe hurried into the room. "You okay?" he asked. "I thought I heard you yell."

"You did," Frank said, rubbing the back of his head. "Whoever was in here knocked me down and got away. But I'm hoping he left some clues behind that will tell us who he was. Come on, help me look."

Together the brothers surveyed the small room. Against the far wall was an electronic board that looked like an eight-track mixer, with lots of levers and dials. Next to it was a computer. "That must be where they program the lasers and sync up the music," Frank said. "Why don't I check that out? You look around the doorway. I scuffled with the guy—maybe he dropped something."

Frank sat down at the computer. He noticed the cover of the processing unit wasn't bolted down. It looked as if it had been removed, then put back in a hurry. He lifted it off and peered into the computer's guts.

Right away he could see that someone had been fooling with the laser motion interface card. It stuck up slightly higher than the other cards, and there were faint pry marks around the ROM chip. Along the top edge of the card were a couple of minute flecks of neon green paint. When Frank saw those, his eyes narrowed.

Just then Joe whooped. "Pay dirt!" he crowed. "Bro, we just got our man. Look at this!"

Frank spun around in his chair. Joe was holding up what looked like a bluish green pebble. "Recognize this?" he asked.

Frank squinted. "Hey—that looks like the stone in Byron's ring!" he exclaimed.

"Uh-huh." Joe nodded. "Must have fallen out of the ring when you two struggled."

"That's right! The guy banged his arm against the door and I heard a clink," Frank recalled. "Well, that stone is evidence, no doubt about it.

And there's more—check this out." He beckoned Joe over to the computer and pointed out the flecks of green paint on the interface card.

"Neon green," Joe noted. "The color of Phil's miniature tools!"

"Yup." Frank's smile was grim. "Remember, Phil said his screwdriver was still missing? Well, it looks as if it was used here. I think we just solved two mysteries. Byron, the electronics whiz, tampered with the laser show, and he also stole and sabotaged Roger!"

Joe sprang up and punched his fist into the air. "We got him," he said triumphantly. "Do you think he's also the one who stole the leash and tried to kill Makowski?"

"Don't know," Frank said, shrugging. "But I think it's time for some hard questions."

The Hardys went back to the skydeck in search of Byron. Phil and Megan were there, wondering what had happened. Joe quickly briefed them, and both friends volunteered to help look.

"Have you seen Byron?" Joe asked a group of girls dancing.

"We wish we had," one giggled. "If you find him, tell him we want him to dance with us."

"Unless *you* want to dance with us," another one said.

Joe grinned. "Some other time," he promised.

When the friends met by the snack table, no one had found Byron.

"Let's go to his room," Frank suggested. "Phil

and Megan can hang out here and catch him if he's still here."

Frank and Joe grabbed a cab and were banging at Byron's door in twenty minutes. They weren't surprised when no one answered. After looking to make sure they were unobserved, Joe slipped a credit card between the door and the frame.

Expertly he maneuvered the plastic. Moments later the lock clicked open, and the Hardys let themselves into Byron's room.

Everything was orderly, almost as if no one was staying there. Quickly they searched the room for clues that might tie Byron into the crimes of the last two days. But they found nothing.

"This place is too clean," Joe said. "I don't trust people who are this neat."

Frank yawned. "I'm beat. Let's call it quits," he suggested. "After all, Byron'll be at the competition tomorrow. That's when the winner will be announced."

"Yeah, Byron would never miss that," Joe agreed. He followed Frank down the hall to their room. "Guess that's when we'll have to bust him."

The next morning the guys missed breakfast. Joe had turned off the alarm, and they had slept an hour too late. When they got to Cahill College, the exhibit hall was already open to the public.

Phil groaned. "There are so many people here today. And look at all those little kids."

"Yeah, but think how many people will see our robot," Frank reminded him.

Phil cracked a smile. He had a weakness for attention. "Let's set Roger up now," he said.

"Come on, Frank," Joe said. "Phil can take care of the robot. We have to deal with Byron."

"Right." Frank fingered Byron's ring stone in his pocket as they hurried toward his booth.

Byron's friend Tess was hanging around his booth, along with a crowd of other teenagers. They all eyed Frank and Joe coldly as the brothers approached.

"Hi, guys!" Byron chirped. "Did you have fun at the laser show last night?"

One or two of his friends snickered.

Joe's blue eyes flashed, but he kept silent when Frank threw him a warning look.

"Byron, is this yours?" Frank asked, holding out the blue-green stone.

Byron's smile was bland. "Sure is! Thanks. I was bummed when I thought I'd lost it," he said, and held out his hand.

Frank didn't give him the stone. "We found it in the laser programming room," he said.

"Really?" Byron said. "I wonder how it got there."

"I think you know," Joe growled. "My brother knocked it off your ring when you attacked him in the dark after sabotaging the lasers."

"Heavy accusation!" Byron sneered. "But finding my stone there doesn't prove anything. Anyone could have found it and planted it."

"I can prove you were there," Frank said quietly. "Please empty your pockets."

"My—my pockets?" Byron suddenly looked uncertain.

"That's right." Joe grinned as he caught on. "Empty 'em right now. Unless you're afraid?"

Byron looked around. His friends were staring at him, waiting to see what he'd do.

"I'm not afraid," he blustered, and dug his hands into his pants pockets. Soon his wallet, a key ring, and some change lay on the booth table.

"Coat pockets, too," Frank said.

Scowling, Byron reached for his long wool coat. He stuck a hand in the right pocket, then pulled it out. "Nothing in there," he said.

Joe caught his arm quickly. "But what's that up your sleeve?" he asked, shaking Byron's arm.

A small metal object shot out and rolled to Frank's feet. He picked it up. It was Phil's miniature screwdriver!

Frank held it up in front of Byron's sulky face. "This is ours," he said. "You stole it when you stole our robot. And you used it on the interface card last night. Too bad for you some of the green paint from the handle chipped off on the edge of the card."

After a second Byron gave an obnoxious laugh. "Guys, guys! So I fooled around with some lasers

111

and rigged your robot's remote. It was all a joke. You take yourselves so seriously—you're such know-it-alls. I just wanted to shake things up."

"Not funny," Frank said.

"I can't help it if you have no sense of humor," Byron said. "What are you going to do, have me arrested?"

"Not for the sabotage," Joe replied. "But we might tell the police to ask you about the weapon that was used to shoot at Mr. Makowski. The remote control that was installed in that thing looks like your work."

Byron turned pale. "Whoa. Wait a second." He swallowed. "I had nothing to do with that. I swear it. Really. You gotta believe me!"

"Why should we?" Joe shot back.

Frank put a hand on Joe's arm. "Where were you sitting during Makowski's speech?" he asked Byron.

"I wasn't there." Byron looked down, embarrassed. "I was—uh—a little queasy. Boats do that to me. I went down to the dining room and lay down on a sofa behind the piano."

"Did anyone see you?" Frank asked.

Byron shook his head. "I don't think so. Megan Sweetwater was down there, too, but she didn't see me."

Frank and Joe exchanged quick glances. So Byron had seen Megan! That made it seem pretty likely that he was telling the truth. It also meant they finally had proof that whoever Makowski had seen going up the ladder to the observation deck definitely *wasn't* Megan. Put Makowski's story together with the dog hairs in the launcher, and it definitely looked as if someone was trying to frame her.

As a final test, Frank pulled out the note they had found stuck in the door of the closet where Joe had been imprisoned. "What do you know about this?" he challenged, throwing it to Byron.

"That's my paper," Byron said. He unfolded the note and read it. "Hey, guys! I had nothing to do with this! I swear on my life!"

"Well, who else might have had some of your paper?" Joe asked.

"Anyone could have taken it from my machine. I gave some to the judges, too," Byron said. He sounded dazed—all the fight gone out of him.

His story sounded plausible. But Frank wasn't going to let him off the hook yet. Byron had caused the Hardys and Phil a lot of grief over the past two days. It was time for him to sweat a little now.

"Okay, let's go see Makowski and Zorba," Frank said. "You can try your story out on them and see what they think."

Byron's former supporters silently moved away as, with Frank on one side and Joe on the other, he headed for the TIC office. As they walked down the narrow hall toward the stairs, he kept babbling that he had had nothing to do with attacking anyone.

"Quiet. What's that?" Joe asked sharply, when they heard a faint hum droning behind them.

The three guys whirled around. A vehicle like a golf cart was closing in on them. With five feet to go, it was about to plow straight into them! Yueh was at the wheel, his face a complete blank.

"Yueh!" Joe yelled. The guys flattened themselves against the wall.

Yueh didn't answer. Instead, he just slumped in the seat. The car lunged forward.

"He's pressing down the accelerator!" Frank shouted, as the cart whizzed by the guys. It shot on toward the stairs.

"He's going over!" Joe yelled.

12 Rendezvous with Death

With only seconds to act, Joe leapt over the back of the cart into the seat next to Yueh.

"Wha—?" Yueh mumbled. He raised his head groggily as Joe's elbow rammed him in the back. The cart was within feet of flying over the top step.

"Move!" Joe shouted. Reaching over, he yanked Yueh's leg off the accelerator and pushed him toward the open side. At the same time, he jammed his own foot onto the brake.

"It's not going to work!" Joe yelled when the cart only slowed a little. It would never stop before it crashed down the flight of stairs.

Yueh was frozen in his seat. Joe made a split-second decision and dived right into the young inventor. The two boys tumbled off the side in

115

one big tangled mess. Just after they hit the ground, they heard a series of loud crashes.

Joe sat up gingerly. The cart was lying at the bottom of the stairs with its wheels spinning in the air. It was badly bent and smashed.

"You okay?" Frank asked, dashing to his brother's side. "That was fast thinking!"

Joe nodded, speechless. If he and Yueh had gone over with the cart, they would certainly have been injured.

"Oh, no," Yueh moaned from the floor. "I can't believe it." He stood up shakily and stared at the wreck.

"Yueh, you almost killed yourself. You also almost ran us down. Why?" Joe demanded.

Yueh looked shocked. "I must have fallen asleep," he said. "I—I'm so sorry. Man, Carl's going to kill me!" He started wringing his hands.

"Carl's the owner of the cart," Byron explained. "It's his invention. The thing is powered by household garbage."

"What am I going to tell him?" Yueh moaned.

"Why did you have Carl's cart?" Frank asked.

"Uh, I borrowed it," Yueh explained. "I was going to the office to talk to Mr. Zorba. Carl asked me to pick up an extra chair for his booth. I said I would if I could take the cart."

"You said you fell asleep?" Joe asked.

Yueh nodded. "I've had less than two hours sleep since Thursday. First someone steals my invention, and I have to replace it. Then I have to finish my application for Cal Tech—"

Frank broke in. "That's where Tanya goes."

"Yeah." Yueh nodded again. "She's helping me with the application. It's due Monday. I brought my essay here to show Tanya, who does student recruitment for Cal Tech. She said it was all wrong, and she gave me ideas about how to fix it. I spent all last night rewriting it."

"Oh, so you missed all the excitement last night?" Frank asked, watching Yueh's face.

"Excitement? I was at a twenty-four-hour copy shop cuddled up to a time-share computer. Was there a party or something?" Yueh asked.

"There was a huge fire. Someone blew up the hotel safe and stole Megan Sweetwater's leash," Frank explained.

Yueh's eyes widened. "Wow!" he said. "I'm not crazy about Megan, but that really stinks."

Joe was wondering just how much Yueh disliked Megan. Enough to try to frame her for the attack on Makowski?

"Yueh, where were you during the cruise on Thursday night?" Joe asked. "We want a straight answer—no more evasions."

Yueh looked at the ground. "I don't want to get anyone in trouble," he mumbled.

"You'll get yourself in plenty of trouble by not telling the truth," Joe assured him.

"After my invention was stolen, Tanya and I

drove to St. Louis to get my prototype," Yueh said at last. "It took us eight hours round-trip. We left at seven and didn't get back to Chicago until three A.M." He looked up at Frank. "I didn't tell you before because judges aren't supposed to do anything that might be seen as favoring one of the contestants. I swear, Tanya didn't judge my invention any differently than anyone else's—she wouldn't do that. Her going with me to St. Louis was just a favor from a friend. But Makowski's just looking for a chance to throw her off the judges' panel. He hates her."

Joe frowned. "Can you prove that you drove to St. Louis?" he asked.

"Sure!" Yueh said eagerly. "I had to get my physics teacher to let me into the lab, where my prototype was. He'll tell you. We were there!"

Frank looked at Joe, and Joe nodded. They'd check Yueh's story, of course, but it looked as if another suspect had just been eliminated.

Yueh left to tell Carl the bad news about his cart. The Hardys and Byron continued downstairs to the TIC office. Byron still had to make his confession.

When they got to the office, Makowski wasn't around. But Ari Zorba was.

"Why don't you three come in here." Zorba opened the door to the office. The boys followed him in, and he took a seat at the big conference table. Looking at the Hardys, he sighed. "Why do

118

I know you're going to tell me about some more trouble?" he asked.

"We're not the ones who are *making* trouble," Joe retorted. "We're just trying to help."

"Anyway," Frank put in, "this time it's Byron who has something to tell you."

Zorba raised his eyebrows at Byron. "Well?"

"Uh, I'm the one who made the lasers go nuts last night, sir. Sorry." Byron gulped, then hurried on. "Also, I'm the one who sabotaged Frank's robot. I was just, well, trying to liven things up."

Zorba's face turned red with anger. "Mr. Paige, I don't want to hear about *why* you did it," he thundered. "When that robot got out of control, it almost destroyed one of our corporate sponsors' booths. That could have cost millions of dollars of damage—not to mention bad press and an angry sponsor. This is serious business. And that stunt last night—you could have ruined the laser projection equipment. You've had it, mister. You're disqualified from this competition."

Byron looked down at his shoes. "Yes, sir."

Zorba thumbed through the papers on the desk. Then he handed Byron a withdrawal form to fill out.

As Byron wrote, Zorba turned to the Hardys. "Thank you, gentlemen," he said stiffly. "And please don't take it personally if I say I'd rather not have to see you in here again."

Joe bit back a retort, and he and Frank silently left the room.

Back at the booth, they helped Phil pack up Roger. Having skipped breakfast, an early lunch sounded good to them all.

"So what did Makowski say about Byron?" Phil asked after they had gotten their food in the cafeteria.

"Makowski wasn't there, but Zorba was. He made Byron withdraw from the competition," Frank answered. Quickly, he and Joe brought Phil up to date on everything else that had happened and the conclusions they had come to.

"So here's where we stand," Joe summed it up. "We know Byron stole and sabotaged Roger and messed up the lasers. We also know that he didn't shoot at Makowski."

"Byron's story also confirms Megan's alibi about where she was," Frank put in. "Not that we didn't already believe Megan was telling the truth," he added hastily when both Phil and Joe shot him dirty glances. "The point is, we now have even more reason to believe that someone was trying to frame Megan for shooting at Makowski. And that makes me think that the Makowski shooting must be linked to the theft of Megan's leash. I just don't know how." Frowning, he stuffed a forkful of spaghetti into his mouth.

"Tanya and Yueh also seem to be out," Joe said, picking up the discussion again. "I'm going to check their story about driving to St. Louis on Thursday night, but it sounded true to me."

"So who's left?" Phil asked. "Zorba?"

"He's got opportunity," Frank offered.

"I just don't see it," Joe said. "Zorba's a jerk, sure, and he obviously resents Makowski for horning in on his job, but where does Megan come into it?"

"Do you think the whole thing with Megan's leash could just be an elaborate way of setting up a false trail?" Phil asked. "A cover-up?"

Frank shook his head. "No one would go to that much risk. Whoever did all that stuff to Megan could have been caught a dozen times. No, there's got to be some link between Megan's leash and the attempt to kill Makowski." He frowned. An idea was tickling at the back of his mind, but he couldn't bring it into focus.

Joe put his soda can down. "Maybe we ought to see if Megan can help us sort this out."

"I haven't seen her yet today," Phil said. "I guess she didn't want to come to the competition, now that her leash is gone."

"Maybe we should go check on her," Joe said.

Frank nodded. "Phil, if you'd be Roger's sitter, Joe and I will go back to the hotel and see if we can find her."

"Good idea," Phil said.

The Hardys walked briskly to the hotel. In the lobby, the desk clerk stopped them.

121

"Excuse me, aren't you friends of the dark-haired young lady with the dog?" he asked.

Frank and Joe realized they could hear a faint yelping coming from the back hall.

When they said yes, he motioned for them to follow him off to the side. "Do you know where she is today? Normally, in the morning she comes to the animal holding room and feeds her dog at eight. Today she never came. I called her room and got no answer. Her dog's throwing a fit. I fed it, but nearly got attacked in the process. I can't control that beast much longer."

Suddenly worried, Frank looked at Joe. He could see the concern in Joe's eyes, too.

"We're looking for her, too." Joe said quickly. "We'll go up and see if she's in her room. Maybe her phone's off the hook."

The Hardys hurried up to Megan's room. There was no answer to Joe's knocking and calling. Looking both ways, he took out his credit card and deftly opened the door.

The boys stepped into the dark room. Megan wasn't there. Nothing seemed out of place. Then Joe pulled out the drawer where Megan kept her blueprints taped. They were gone!

"Look at this," Frank called grimly. He held up a crumpled piece of paper.

Joe smoothed out the lined piece of paper and read the scrawled words aloud: "'If you want your leash back, meet me at the dock under the

Marina Restaurant at 2 A.M. ALONE. Bring the specs.'"

Both Hardys stared at the clock on the bedside table. It was 10:45. That meant Megan had been missing for almost nine hours.

"We've got to get down to the marina and find her!" Joe said frantically.

Frank didn't add the words he knew were in Joe's mind. *If it isn't already too late!*

13 Failed Rescue

Frank and Joe ran down the stairs. Breathlessly, Joe told the desk clerk that they needed Megan's dog.

When he just stared at them, Frank pounded on the counter. "Look, there's no time to explain. Where's the dog?" he demanded.

Seeing that the boys meant business, the desk clerk led them to Bunny. The big dog jumped all over them, happy to see someone he recognized.

Joe grabbed a red nylon leash he saw hanging behind the door, tied up Bunny, and the Hardys hit the street.

"The dock is only about ten blocks from here, on the Chicago River," Frank said, as they stood on the busy sidewalk trying to get their bearings.

Just then, Nicholas Makowski rounded the block, almost running into the Hardys. Bunny whined and leapt up to lick Makowski's hand.

"Well, hello," Makowski said. "Aren't you a fine fellow!" He looked up at the Hardys. "A great-looking beast huh?"

Joe ignored the question. "Mr. Makowski, Megan is missing. We think she's been kidnapped," he said urgently. He explained about the note they had found.

Makowski whistled. "Good lord! This is very serious. Have you called the police?"

"No time to explain it all to them," Frank replied.

"You boys go ahead. I'll call the police immediately." Makowski turned toward the hotel.

"Tell them to be careful," Joe urged. "If Megan's kidnapper sees any police around, there's no telling what'll happen!"

"Don't worry," Makowski assured him. "I know just how to handle them."

The brothers headed north on the street. Where the Chicago River split, they followed Wacker Drive toward Lake Michigan. Joe shivered when the brisk wind cut through his jacket.

A few minutes later, the Hardys were standing across the river from the Marina Restaurant. The top floor of the tattered, bleak building jutted out toward the water. The old red letters in the sign drooped, and the R had already fallen off. Several

125

windows were boarded up. The bottom portion of the building, with its huge iron door, seemed to be a warehouse loading bay.

"Very nice," Joe muttered. "For a criminal, that is."

"We have to get across the river and figure out how to get down to the docks," Frank said.

They crossed the nearby crowded bridge. On the other side, Joe stopped and peered over the thick wall onto the riverbank.

"I don't see how we're supposed to get down there," he muttered, looking at the building.

"There must be stairs somewhere. The people who used these docks needed some way to get up," Frank said. "Look." He pointed to a flight of worn stone steps that led to the river.

The Hardys jumped the chain blocking the crumbling stairs and pulled the whimpering Bunny under after them.

"Careful! There's a lot of mold on these things. Don't slip," Frank warned.

Bunny sat on the steps, refusing to move. "Heel, Bunny!" Joe commanded. The cringing dog nudged up against Joe's leg and reluctantly stumbled after him.

"It's wet," Frank cautioned when they reached the narrow platform at the bottom. Avoiding the waves that lapped onto the decaying cement, they ran to the wider dock in front of the warehouse.

Frank shivered. The air felt damp, heavy, and

stale. A pile of wooden boards rotted against the warehouse door.

"Megan can't still be around here. There's nowhere to *be,* at least that I see. There's no room behind those boards. That rusty chain on the door hasn't moved for decades," Joe said as he surveyed the dock.

"Let Bunny loose," Frank said. "Maybe he'll be able to pick up her smell. Let's look for any clues to what happened down here."

Joe released the dog. Bunny sat on his haunches looking forlorn.

"He'll move," Frank said confidently. He patted the dog as he passed. "Look at all this dust. No one's been down here for a long time."

"Hey," Joe called from over by the warehouse door. "There are footprints over here!"

A large pair and a smaller pair of fresh footprints were left in the thick dust. Frank followed them over to the pile of boards. All of a sudden, the prints disappeared into patternless dust streaks.

"Joe, look at the marks on the floor. The dust is all messed up over here. Looks like there was a struggle."

Bunny crawled over to the guys. When he got closer, he started whimpering.

"What's with the mutt?" Joe asked, watching the dog nose around the rotting wood. Bunny scratched the cement with his paws and whined.

"Why can't you talk, pup?" Joe complained.

The dog started circling the boards, yelping and barking as he ran back and forth.

"There's something about those boards," Frank said as he peered into the pile.

"Look!" Joe cried. "See that shiny thing under there?" He dug into the pile and pulled out a key. Dangling from it was a plastic key chain with the number 418 on it.

"Megan's new room number," Frank said. "Is there anything else in there?"

Joe crouched back down. Excitedly he pushed a plank aside. Underneath, barely showing, was the corner of a dull metal plate.

Frank grabbed the two planks that were covering it. He pulled them over to the side. Now they could see a rusty ring in the middle of the metal square.

"It's a trapdoor," Joe breathed.

"It must lead to a basement of some sort," Frank said. He grasped the rusty ring in the middle and tried to pull up the plate, but it wouldn't budge. "We need something to run through the ring to get more leverage."

"What about this?" Joe suggested. He carried over a thick metal rod he had found in the corner and stuck it through the loop. Using the ground for leverage, he pried the plate up.

The door flipped open and crashed backward onto the cement. He peered into the trapdoor opening. Stairs led down into darkness. A foul, mildewy smell blasted into the guys' faces.

"Ugh!" Joe gagged at the smell. "Let's tie up the dog and get down there."

Bunny was whining loudly. He walked up to the trapdoor, barked, and ran back cringing. As Joe tied his leash to a ring on the warehouse door, the dog trembled and cried.

"The dog's flipping out. Megan's got to be down there," Frank said, leading the way down the narrow steps.

They groped along the wall, using Frank's little penlight until their eyes adjusted to the darkness. At the bottom, they made out the outlines of the stone walls of the basement. They could still hear Bunny whining above them.

"Megan? Are you down here?" Joe called.

His voice echoed eerily. The only answer was the sound of water lapping against the walls.

"We must be under the river's surface," Frank said slowly. "See those metal plates on the wall? They look as if they used to be windows. This place was above water at some point. Then either the water level rose, or the place sank."

"Listen," Joe said sharply.

There was a faint rustling sound.

"What is that?" Joe asked.

Frank crept across the room. "It's coming from over here," he called over his shoulder.

As they moved deeper into the basement, they saw that there was an archway in the wall that opened into another room.

The rustling got louder as they approached.

129

Frank sidled up to the wall and motioned for his brother to do the same on the other side of the arch. Slowly Frank stuck his head around the archway to see what was in the next room. A black form struggled in the corner. It was Megan! She was on her knees, tied and gagged, desperately trying to loosen the ropes.

The Hardys ran over to her. She looked up with petrified eyes.

"It's okay," Frank said softly. "We'll have you out in a second." They quickly untied her.

"Thanks," she said hoarsely as they helped her stand and get her circulation going again.

"Did you see whoever put you down here?" Frank asked urgently.

Megan shook her head. "H-he came up behind me," she mumbled. She was trembling uncontrollably. Looking at her, the Hardys knew that now wasn't the time to ask her questions.

"Hey, your dog's waiting for you," Joe said as cheerfully as he could. "He helped us find you. I guess he's not so bad after all."

Megan smiled bravely and tried to take a step forward. Frank and Joe each gave her an arm, and the trio moved slowly toward the trapdoor.

They could hear Bunny barking. Suddenly the barks turned to whines. Then there was a single sharp yip. Then silence.

"Bunny! What's wrong? I have to get to him!" Megan cried, tottering forward.

Joe leapt and caught her arm as she nearly fell.

"Easy," he said. He pointed to the light streaming in through the trapdoor. "Look, we're almost there."

At that moment the door crashed shut.

"What the—?" Frank ran up the narrow steps, groping in the blackness until he felt the cold metal door. He pushed up on the plate with all his strength. It didn't budge.

Joe left Megan leaning on the wall. He joined his brother at the top of the stairs. With his shoulder to the plate, he pushed with Frank. Nothing moved.

"Again," Frank grunted. "One, two—"

On three, his voice was drowned out by a creaking, tearing noise. A second later Joe's stomach cramped up when he heard the sound of water gushing into the room.

"Oh, no!" Megan yelled. "Oh, no!"

The Hardys turned slowly, prepared for the worst. One of the metal sheets boarding up the old windows was sagging away, torn loose from its fastening at an upper corner. Frigid river water pulsed through the ragged metal edges of the hole, falling into the basement. Already, two inches of water rippled on the floor. On the water floated a stubby Lucite arrow.

"Oh, no," Megan said again, this time in a whisper. "We're going to drown!"

14 Cold, Wet Pressure

"Get on the steps," Frank called over the noise of the falling water. Megan scrambled up the stairs, next to the Hardys. Her feet were soaked.

Joe took a deep breath. "Let's try the trapdoor again. Megan, you help," he ordered briskly.

Crowded onto an upper stair, the three teens heaved up against the cold metal plate.

"Again!" Frank shouted, when the door seemed to quiver slightly. "Come on, guys. I think it moved."

Together they rammed it with all their strength. The door stayed perfectly still this time.

Megan started sobbing. "We're never going to get out of here!" she cried as the tears flowed down her cheeks.

Neither Frank nor Joe had the confidence to

tell her that everything would be fine. Grimly, they shoved up against the door again.

When nothing happened, the Hardys sank down on the cold steps.

"There's got to be a way," Frank said in a low, tired voice.

Joe and Megan just looked at him. The water was already creeping up to the third step. In half an hour, they would be dead.

Joe jumped off the stairs, plunging thigh-deep into the freezing water. He started wading around the room, desperately searching for anything that might help them get out.

"Hey, Frank," Joe yelled suddenly. The echo sounded strange, bouncing off the surface of the water. "There are some more metal poles down in this corner. Let's ram one against the door. Maybe our concentrated force will do it."

Frank pushed through the water to Joe's side. Together they brought two heavy, rusted poles over to the steps. The water was already lapping over the fifth step. Only nine more to go.

"At the count of three, shove as hard as you can," Joe instructed. They pushed up with the pole. The heavy door bounced up a couple inches, then slammed down hard.

Frank wiped his gritty forehead. "We can do this!" he shouted, encouragingly. Again, they rammed the door. The same thing happened.

"We can't get the door up high enough. It's

never going to flip open," Megan wailed. Frank glanced at the shaking girl. After all she'd been through, there was no way she'd have the strength to shove the pole again.

More water was seeping into their shoes. The floor was flooded up to the sixth step.

Thinking quickly, Frank handed the second pole to Megan. She could barely hold it steady.

"Megan, Joe and I will ram the door up again. You get up on the top step. When the door bounces up, jam your pole into the crack, so that it holds the door open. Then we'll use leverage to pry the door all the way open," Frank shouted above the crashing water.

Megan nodded and climbed as high as she could without hitting her head on the door. She held the heavy pole in a ready position.

"Okay," she shouted.

Frank and Joe tensed their muscles. Together, they pushed up as hard as they could. The door bounced up. With a yell, Megan slid her pole forward and into the crack.

The Hardys cheered when the door bounced back down and they could still see light from the outside. The pole had kept the door from slamming shut again.

"Good work!" Joe yelled.

Megan was leaning against the wall, exhausted. The two boys stepped up and grabbed her pole. They pushed it about halfway through the crack. Using it like a crowbar, they leaned all their weight against their end. As the other end rose, the door started lifting.

"A little more," Frank groaned. When he thought his arms were going to melt like silly putty, the door hit the midpoint and fell open.

Joe reached back and grabbed Megan's hand. Pulling her up, the three teens climbed the last few steps and crawled up onto the warehouse dock.

The three sat on the cold cement in silence.

"That was too close," Joe finally said. He stood up and looked down the trapdoor. The water level was two feet below the dock.

"Where's Bunny?" Megan said in a strangled voice. "Bunny! Come, pup!"

Quickly Frank jumped to his feet. "Bunny," he called as he walked over to the warehouse door where the dog had been tied. The leash and dog were gone.

Just then Joe cleared his throat. He was standing by the pile of rotting wood. "Bunny's over here," he said quietly, shooting a warning look to Frank.

Megan turned slowly. "Something's wrong," she said in a chilly voice. "He would have come to me when I called."

Wordlessly, Joe went to Megan and led her to the woodpile. Frank followed with a bad feeling in the pit of his stomach.

Bunny was stretched on his side. A stubby arrow stuck out of the animal's shoulder.

Megan made a strange, garbled noise. "He's dead!" she cried. She dropped to her knees.

Just then Bunny drew in a long, labored breath. And another. Megan's eyes shone with tears of relief. "Maybe he'll be okay," she whispered.

As she gently stroked her dog, Frank reached down and carefully pulled the arrow out. He ripped a piece of cloth off his shirt and pressed it to the wound to stop the small trickle of blood. "It doesn't look too deep," he reported.

"Let's get him out of here," Joe said. He and Frank tied their jackets together and lifted the dog into the makeshift sling.

Then the Hardys, with Bunny between them and Megan following, exhausted, climbed back up to the street level. They caught a cab to the hotel.

In the lobby, Tanya was talking to a student. When she saw the wet, dirty, shivering teens walk in, she gasped and came running over.

"What happened?" she cried.

"Quick, call a vet," Joe said. He and Frank carefully lowered Bunny to the carpet. Without questions, Tanya hurried to the phone at the front desk.

Leaving Megan with her pet, the Hardys went to change clothes. When they got back to the lobby, Tanya was sitting with Megan. "The vet's on his way," Tanya announced.

After a brief argument, the Hardys convinced

Megan to leave Bunny long enough to change into dry clothes. She stumbled off to her room.

"Too bad Makowski's not around," Tanya commented. "He's a dog expert."

Frank stared at Tanya. "What do you mean?"

"Didn't you know? He's a pedigree breeder on the side," she answered. "It's his passion."

Frank suddenly got a faraway look in his eyes. He was silent for a long moment.

"Frank?" Joe said, waving a hand in front of his brother's face.

"Where is Makowski now?" Frank asked slowly.

"At the competition, I guess," Tanya answered, shrugging. "He missed a session earlier. Zorba was furious."

"Why aren't you there?" Joe asked.

Tanya's smile was bitter. "Didn't you hear? Makowski threw me out. For giving Yueh an unfair advantage."

"The police never did come," Frank murmured suddenly.

"What?" Joe started to say. But then, suddenly, he saw exactly what Frank was getting at. "Oh, wow," he breathed. "You think—"

Frank nodded tensely. "It's the only answer that fits."

"What?" Tanya demanded. "What are you guys talking about?"

Ignoring the question, Joe jumped to his feet. "We've got to catch him," he said to Frank.

"Let's go," Frank agreed. He turned to Tanya. "Do us one more favor. Call the police and tell them to meet us at Cahill College auditorium right away."

When the Hardys got out of the lobby and onto the street, Joe burst out, "It's Makowski, isn't it! How could we have missed it for so long?"

Dodging the other people on the sidewalk, Frank started jogging toward the college. "It has to be. He saw us leave to find Megan. He could have followed us, shut the trapdoor, and used that arrow to bust the rusty window. If Megan's leash was good enough to make millions, he'd know—he's a dog breeder and a corporate engineer."

"And he would have known what Megan's invention was and where to reach her way before the contest," Joe added.

Frank nodded. "It all makes sense when you think about it," he said, panting slightly as he jogged. "Everything fits. Makowski's got the know-how and the connections to make a bundle on Megan's invention—if he can cut her out of the deal. But remember, stealing her leash was not his only job."

"He also had to make her look like a criminal, so that no one would listen to her when she claimed he stole her invention," Joe chimed in. "That's why he set up that fake attempt on his own life, then tried to incriminate her."

"Right," Frank agreed. His breath came out in

frosty puffs. "And it almost worked," he added ruefully. "For a while I really wasn't sure about Megan. She was acting so crazy and hostile that I thought she really might have tried to kill Makowski."

"I was never in doubt," Joe said with a trace of smugness. The brothers turned up the walk to the college auditorium, which was in the same complex of buildings as the gymnasium.

After a moment, Joe snapped his fingers and said, "We should have been tipped off by that bogus story he told me about hitting his hand on the rail when he fell overboard. You don't wear a bandage like that on a bruise. I should have remembered—Megan said she bit the hand of the guy who stuffed her in the rocket."

"There were plenty of clues, if you just knew where to look," Frank replied.

They went inside and paused by the heavy oak doors of the auditorium to catch their breath. Through the doors came the sound of clapping.

Joe eyed the wall clock. "It's just about time for Makowski to begin speaking," he said. "Sounds like the place is packed. He won't be expecting to see us again. What do you say we give him a little surprise?"

Frank grinned. "You take that side," he directed, moving to another set of doors. "I'll take this one."

Giving his brother the thumbs-up sign, Joe pulled his doors open and moved into the back of the theater. When Frank opened the doors on his side, the hinges creaked loudly.

Frank felt stares on him as people turned to see who'd come in so late. Makowski looked straight at him. The chairman grabbed the podium. His face turned the color of Swiss cheese as his eyes locked with Frank's.

"Stay right there, Makowski!" Joe's voice rang out from the other aisle.

The audience was starting to murmur. Makowski glanced behind him. Then, turning, he walked rapidly off into the wings.

"Stop him!" Frank yelled. "He's getting away!"

15 Justice
Triumphs

Frank and Joe sprinted down the aisles toward the stage. They were going so fast they didn't see Phil stand up from his seat in the first row and hurry toward a row of inventions on a table near the stage.

The audience was in a complete uproar by now. The Hardys leapt onto the stage and disappeared behind the dark backdrop. Joe flipped on a light switch he found along the wall.

Harsh fluorescent lights hummed and flickered on. The small backstage area was empty except for a few boxes filled with old stage equipment. Makowski was nowhere to be seen.

"That way." Frank pointed to a small door with a burnt-out red neon Exit sign.

Joe raced after him into a narrow hall. The

Hardys ran down to the other end and slammed through a set of doors with crash bars.

"Hey!" Joe said. The corridor connected to the gymnasium!

Through the windows the wintery afternoon light was fast fading into dusk. The gym was shadowed and still. "Split up," Frank whispered. He waved Joe toward the left-side aisles.

Joe crept cautiously down the farthest aisle. Every nerve was on edge. Makowski had already tried to kill them once. He was a desperate man, and there was no telling what he would do if he was cornered.

He rounded a corner and started up the next aisle. Too late, he became aware of the presence behind him. Before he could even move, he felt the metal edge of a cylinder pressed into his back between his shoulder blades.

"Know what this is?" Makowski whispered in his ear. "It's my launcher. You know what it can do. So I'd be good if I were you, son."

Joe nodded slightly. "Okay," he murmured.

"Frank Hardy!" Makowski called. "I've got your brother! Come out where I can see you."

When Frank didn't answer, Makowski nudged Joe with the launcher. "Tell him," he snarled.

"It's true," Joe said in a dejected tone.

A moment later Frank moved out from behind a booth. He held his hands out in front of him to show Makowski they were empty.

"Do you really think you can get away with

this?" Frank asked. "Everyone saw us chasing you after you ran off the stage. How long do you think it'll take them to figure it all out?"

Makowski scowled. "Shut up. I'm thinking," he commanded.

"Don't think too long," Frank told him. "The cops will be here soon. Look, you don't have a chance. So why don't you just hand me the weapon and let Joe go."

"Hah!" Makowski jerked Joe's arm up behind his back. Joe winced at the pain. "You two have caused me nothing but trouble. You think I'd let you go now? Oh, no! I'm taking you with me.

"Yeah, that's it!" Makowski went on, smiling wolfishly. "They won't come after me as long as I've got a couple of hostages."

Frank shot a worried glance at Joe. Makowski sounded pretty irrational. Obviously, logic wasn't going to work on him. Joe and Frank exchanged a desperate glance that said, What do we do now?

There was a faint rustle behind Joe, then a familiar whirring noise. Maybe it isn't so hopeless after all, Joe thought. He'd recognize that sound anywhere—it was Roger!

"What's that?" Makowski cried, spinning around with his weapon still in Joe's back.

Suddenly Joe saw an orange blur fly by his face. Roger's ball! Makowski let out a startled yell and aimed the launcher at it. The ball hit Makowski squarely in the chest.

That was all Joe needed. Wrenching his arm out of the tall man's grasp, he spun around and planted a solid right cross to Makowski's chin. Makowski reeled backward, then tried to aim the launcher at Joe. But this time Frank was ready. He sprang forward and swept the launcher from Makowski's hand with one swift, scything kick.

After that it was simple. Joe stepped in with a haymaker and Makowski went down for the count. Joe stood back, blowing on his knuckles.

"Nice one!" came Phil's voice. The Hardys' friend stepped out from behind one of the booth dividers. In his hand was Roger's remote.

"Phil!" Joe clapped him on the back, beaming. "I never thought I'd be so glad to see one of your inventions in my life. Thanks!"

"Man, you saved us!" Frank put in with a sigh. His muscles felt like Jell-O.

"You should be thanking Roger," Phil told them. He patted the robot's head proudly.

"Great serve, Roger!" Frank joked.

"But where'd you come from?" Joe asked Phil.

"When I saw you running after Makowski, I figured he must be our bad guy. I thought you might need some help so"—Phil shrugged—"I brought Roger along. It was the only thing I could think of at the moment," he added.

Just then the gym door burst open. Two blue-clad police officers ran in.

"Hey, the police are here!" Frank exclaimed,

grinning. "Over here, officers." He pointed to Makowski, who was beginning to stir on the floor.

It was nearly eight o'clock by the time the Hardys and Phil finished at the police station and returned to the hotel. When they walked into the lobby, the first person they saw was Megan. Rushing up to them, she whooped ecstatically. Tanya and Yueh were right behind her.

"Everyone's talking about how you busted Makowski!" Megan exclaimed. "Okay, spill! Tell me everything. Are you guys okay?"

"You bet. Didn't I tell you before it's hard to get rid of us?" Joe joked.

Bunny wobbled toward them, thumping his tail and barking. Frank patted the dog.

"The dart was just a tranquilizer," Megan explained. "But the poor baby's still groggy."

"Uh-oh, don't look now," Joe muttered suddenly, "but here comes Mr. Sunshine."

Frank turned around. Ari Zorba was approaching them. He smiled stiffly and held out a hand. Surprised, Frank shook it.

"I just wanted to thank you boys," Zorba said in a gruff voice. "I don't have all the details yet, but I understand that Nick Makowski was behind all the shenanigans at this year's competition." He sniffed. "Can't say I ever liked the man much."

145

"You don't like anyone much," Joe muttered.

"I heard that," Zorba growled. Then his face relaxed into a smile. "And let me say I'm sorry. It isn't that I disliked you boys. It's just that I had a lot on my mind, and I didn't want to listen to a bunch of teenagers telling me how to do my job." His smile broadened. "Although I guess I should have, eh?"

Everyone burst out laughing.

"Anyway, thanks again," Zorba said. "Now, I'm sure you kids would rather talk without an old grouch like me hanging around, so I'll leave you to it." He turned and strode away.

Joe gazed after him. "That guy has style," he said admiringly. "Maybe I misjudged him."

"Hey," Phil said, elbowing Joe in the ribs. "Don't misjudge this. It's almost eight-thirty, and I haven't eaten since noon. I'm starved!"

"And I want to hear about this case," Megan reminded the Hardys. "Come on, let's go out and celebrate!"

The Hardys, Phil, and Megan still had the two gift certificates that the hotel manager had given each of them after the break-in at Megan's room, so they decided to treat Tanya and Yueh to dinner at the fancy restaurant down the street. After they had ordered their food, Frank continued the explanation of Makowski's crimes.

"See, the whole thing makes sense if you just know how to look at it," he said earnestly. "But we were looking at it the wrong way around."

"I'm lost already," Tanya confessed.

Frank smiled. "Today at lunch, Phil almost solved the case. Remember, Phil, you asked if the attacks on Megan and the theft of the leash could all be red-herring crimes to hide the true crime, which was the attempt to kill Makowski?"

Phil nodded. "And you shot me down."

"Well, you were wrong," Frank said. "But the idea was a good one. See, it was the other way around—the attack on Makowski was the real red herring. It was meant to discredit Megan. It was part of a whole campaign to make her look paranoid and unstable, so that when he stole her invention no one would listen to her."

"Wow." Megan looked slightly sick. "I didn't know my leash was so valuable."

"You also have to figure that Makowski is a little unbalanced," Joe told her gently. "He had to be to go to all that trouble for one product."

"But he must have had other people working with him," Megan said suddenly. "What about the woman who called me in New Mexico and again in my hotel room?"

"I think I can explain that," Tanya said. "Makowski's an engineer, don't forget. He has all sorts of electronic toys, including a computer gadget that can alter a speaker's voice. It hooks up to a phone. I saw it in Makowski's office last summer at Fleche, his company."

The waiter arrived with their food just then. When he had served it and left, Joe peered at

Tanya. "Just out of curiosity, what happened between you and Makowski at Fleche?" he asked.

Tanya's face clouded. "He stole one of my ideas," she answered, "and threatened to ruin my career if I ever told anyone about it."

"You never told me that," Yueh broke in, outraged. "You just said it was personal."

"I couldn't tell you," Tanya reminded him. "I took Makowski's threat seriously."

"You were right," Frank told her. "He's a ruthless, determined man.

"Determined enough to arrange his own attempted murder," he went on. "Makowski set up that shooting. He rigged the remote control and altered the launcher to take arrows. He also set Megan up with a bogus phone call so that she'd be on the scene of the crime when it happened. That didn't work, but not because he didn't try."

"Makowski fired the shot at himself—the remote must have been in his pocket," Joe said, taking up the story. "When I think about it now, I remember that he moved aside right *before* the shot was fired. Then he threw himself overboard. That was a big risk he took."

"Yeah, he had no guarantee that someone like you would dive in after him," Phil put in, speaking through a mouthful of steak.

Joe shrugged. "Anyway, the risk paid off. One of the things he accomplished was to prevent us from ever considering him as a suspect—even when he made some mistakes that should have tipped us off."

"Like what?" Megan wanted to know.

"Like telling me to leave the launcher with him before I ever told him about it," Joe replied. "He couldn't have known about it—unless he was the one who had stolen it from Yueh."

"And like attacking Joe when Joe was bringing the launcher to him," Frank added. "He was the only one who knew when Joe had it. But he couldn't let it be handed over to him officially because then he'd have to give it to the police, and they might start asking awkward questions."

"So he jumped me and locked me in a broom closet with a note designed to throw suspicion on Byron Paige," Joe said. "By this time he was getting nervous. He was just trying to spread the suspicion around—he knew we weren't going for his attempt to lay all the blame on Megan."

Megan smiled gratefully. "Thanks," she said. "I can't believe that man actually tied me up and put me in that rocket," Megan went on. "I thought I was being taken hostage or something. You're awfully lucky that rocket didn't fall right on you, Frank."

"Anyway"—Frank swallowed the last of his baked potato—"Makowski's next move was to blow up the hotel safe and steal the leash. We don't know exactly how, but obviously he managed it. Detective Novello's team found the leash, by the way," he added, looking at Megan. "It was in the trunk of Makowski's car."

"I don't know if I really want it back after all this," Megan murmured.

"Come on," Joe teased. "I'm sure Bunny misses it already."

"Makowski still needed the specs for the leash, though," Frank said. "So he sent you that ransom note, Megan." He cleared his throat. "By that time he had also decided that the only way to deal with you was to get rid of you."

"Cold blooded," Yueh said.

"Very," Frank agreed.

Megan grinned. "But once again, he didn't count on you guys." Leaning forward, she put a hand on each Hardy's arm. "My heroes!"

For once, even Joe seemed embarrassed by all the praise. "It was no big deal," he muttered, then quickly changed the subject. "Hey, who won the competition, anyway?"

"We canceled the awards ceremony in light of what happened. Instead, Zorba just announced the winner over the loudspeaker," Tanya explained.

"Yeah. It was some kid we never even heard of," Phil added. "Can you believe it?"

"Man!" Joe struck the table with his palm. "It doesn't seem fair. Megan didn't even get to present at the semifinals—she was tied up in a warehouse while they were going on."

"Calm down," Tanya said with a grin. "Megan gets to make a special presentation tomorrow morning. If we judges like her work, we'll offer her a special prize."

By the end of the evening, everyone was full, happy, and exhausted. They had the kitchen make a steak-filled doggy bag for Bunny. Then they all trooped back to the hotel and said their goodbyes.

The Hardys and Phil caught an eight o'clock flight back to Bayport the next morning. After they had been in the air a while, Joe poked his slumbering brother in the ribs.

"Wake up, it's ten-thirty. Megan's probably back from her presentation." He grinned. "Shall we call her?" he asked, pointing to the credit card–operated phone above the seat.

Phil and Frank laughed. "Let's do it," Frank said, and pulled out his card.

"Hey, Megan," he said, when she answered. "This is your call from thirty-five thousand feet over Cleveland. How'd you do with the leash?"

She laughed. "You guys are crazy!" she said loudly enough for all of them to hear. "Guess what! The judges loved me! The one from the Femtrott company offered me a summer internship. He said if that worked out, the company might be able to send me to college, too."

Joe grabbed the phone. "Congratulations, Sweetwater," he shouted, laughing.

"Hey," Megan told him. "I've got this great idea for next year's competition. See—"

"Stop!" Joe interrupted. "I don't want to hear it. Megan, haven't you learned yet that inventing is hazardous to your health?"